He averted his eyes, shading them with his hand. "Did you know you're…"

"A ghost?" came her bright voice.

"Naked." He risked a peek.

She looked down at herself. "Ah, that. Not much I can do about it, I'm afraid. Not much I can do about being a ghost, either." She folded her arms over her bosom and crossed her legs. "Is this better?"

He carefully looked up. "A little. Would you like a robe or something?"

She shook her head. "Won't do me any good. I can't touch anything solid. Believe me, I've tried."

He knew her, now that he had a chance to look at her without embarrassment or the rushing of blood away from his head. "You're the Stoweham Ghost."

She smiled. "I am."

She was also the woman he'd dreamed of since his adolescence. Not true, solid dreams, but rather catching a glimpse of her just before he awakened. Not that he ever saw her when he was fully conscious. "Have you been haunting me?"

Her gaze slid sideways. "I wouldn't call it haunting. But yes. Then again, I haunt everyone who comes to Stoweham House."

James' head spun. He had to sit down. He eased a chair on the far side of the table and fell into it, letting his head fall into his hands. "Why me?"

She smiled and scooted closer. He scooted back, averting his eyes from her bouncing bosoms. As a young man, he'd dreamed about reaching out and caressing those bosoms. Now his shame flooded back to him.

"Because," she said, "I like you."

The White Feather

by

Heidi Wessman Kneale

This is a work of fiction. Names, characters, places, and incidents are either the product of the author's imagination or are used fictitiously, and any resemblance to actual persons living or dead, business establishments, events, or locales, is entirely coincidental.

The White Feather

Cover Art by *Kristian Norris*

The Wild Rose Press, Inc.
PO Box 708
Adams Basin, NY 14410-0708
Visit us at www.thewildrosepress.com

Publishing History
First Fantasy Rose Edition, 2016
Print ISBN 978-1-5092-0890-6
Digital ISBN 978-1-5092-0891-3

Published in the United States of America

Dedication

For Their Ladyships,
Lady Sarah and Lady Amy:
Courage is not what others see,
but what you see within yourself.

Chapter 1
The Stoweham Ghost

James Cowper's hand shook as he reached for the knob of the Stoweham Community Hall door. He released it and wiped his sweaty palm on his smart gray sack coat, quite fashionable if one was a civilian. On his wide lapel, his hand brushed past the Silver War Badge all men wore if they had failed to pass enlistment or had been sent home from the war.

The Silver War Badge wasn't just a pin. It was a shield against the social scorn of those whose duty it was to shame able-bodied men to enlist. For most men, it kept them safe.

For James, nothing could keep him safe. He'd walked all the way from Stoweham House to the Community Hall that afternoon, a good mile-and-a-half. In that time, he'd received no less than two white feathers from hoity-toity young ladies who disregarded his Silver War Badge.

In the village of Stoweham, James Cowper had been branded a coward. No badge, no letter from the War Office, nothing could erase that stain.

Still, James had to try. To not try would be to prove their opinions correct.

So why was it so difficult to open a simple wooden door and walk into the Stoweham Community Hall? It shouldn't take all his gumption to say, "I want to join the Volunteer Training Corps." Indeed, if a man wasn't off fighting for King and Country, it was his duty to join the Volunteer Training Corps. The Great War demanded all the men Britannia had to offer.

The Corps were little more than the too young or too old, or other men unsuitable for the manly art of war. Not that the Stoweham VTC would be effective, should Jerry invade Britain's fair shores. They were better equipped to defending their own patriotism than their country.

Still, one must do one's duty. Pushing all thoughts out of his head, James opened the door.

The VTC meeting had already started. A motley group of men and boys sat in rows of wooden folding chairs, facing an old chalkboard. James lowered his gaze and hurried in, hoping no one would notice him. Perhaps he could slip into the back row and remain hidden?

No. A gust of wind caught the door, shutting it with a loud clunk. James jumped.

"Well, lookee here." Billy Forsythe, who had been standing at the chalkboard, scoffed at him. "Look who's come to join us, lads."

At the sound of Billy's voice, as one, every single man in that room turned to look at James.

His stomach sank. Of all the people in Stoweham, Billy Forsythe was the one who stuck into him most. He and Billy went way back, and not in a nice way. Billy was one of those heavyset lads with a round nose and thick fingers that betrayed his common Anglo Saxon stock. Proud of it too, he was. While he was not taller than James, Billy had had no compunction pushing the slimmer James around as lads. Adulthood had not changed him.

Billy, who was two years older than James, had been one of the first to enlist. Most of the other Stoweham men had followed. Billy was also one of the first to return. He had taken a nasty tree splinter in the left hand from a close-call with a hand grenade. The hand had turned septic and needed amputation, thus leaving him unsuitable for military duty. Billy didn't need a Silver War Badge. His missing hand was badge enough. He displayed it proudly, with his coat sleeve pushed up and his shirt cuff buttoned back. While some of the more delicate ladies of the village would wish he had the decency to cover up, Billy refused to hide his pride.

James drew himself up. He might have been slender, but he would not let Billy see that he was intimidated. "Why wouldn't I? It's my duty." Did his voice have to sound so weak? He forced one foot in front of another, intending to sit in the nearest vacant chair. He'd forgotten his hat; he drew it off, now that he was indoors.

"Glad you volunteered," said Billy.

But as James descended to the seat, Billy said, "What are you doing? I said you volunteered."

"What?"

"Come on up to the front." Billy's lips twitched with smugness.

The men around him murmured to their pals. James looked around, a trepidation filling him.

Then his gaze fell upon the chalkboard. There, in shaky, hand-drawn lines, was the outline of a rifle.

Spots appeared before his eyes. Of all the days to come, he came for the firearm lecture? His heart rate increased, and his palms broke out in a fierce sweat.

Billy sneered. "Oh, come now. You've handled a rifle before."

He had, when he was fourteen. Of course Billy knew. Billy had been there, as had several other lads.

Things did not end well that day.

A slight tremor affected his hands. Memories of his time in the recruitment office in Buckingham flooded back.

He drew a deep breath. No, he would not faint. Not again. He rose to his feet and came forward. "We've all handled a rifle," James replied.

Billy humphed and smacked a hand on the blackboard. A small puff of chalk flew out from his impact. "So, tell us the parts."

Now the cold sweat ran down his face. He did his best to control his voice. "Butt, stock, barrel, striker, trigger, bolt, bolt head..." His finger pointed to each part on the crude illustration. Just because he feared handling a rifle didn't mean he didn't know its parts.

"Not bad," Billy said, his voice full of mockery. "Let's see how you do with a real one."

In one swift action, Billy tossed James a real rifle. Where'd he get it? James could have sworn there wasn't one before. Had he been hiding it, waiting in anticipation of surprising James?

His hands wanted to catch the object tossed at him. His heart wanted his feet to run away. With such mixed signals, he failed to catch it fully. It fumbled in his hands before clattering to the ground.

"Take cover!" Billy shouted. All the men dove off their chairs to huddle on the ground.

Spots appeared before James' eyes, and he reached

for the weapon. It would do no good if it went off and accidentally killed someone. He recovered it without incident, but how his hands shook! He hadn't held a rifle since his last attempt to enlist last year.

That did not turn out well either.

Billy had risen to his feet. "You bloody idiot!" he shouted right in James' face. He snatched the rifle away. "You could have gotten us all killed."

Without warning, he swung the butt of the rifle around at James' head. James ducked only enough so the butt glanced off his skull. Still, that hurt. When Billy swung the rifle around again for another blow, James delivered a punch to Billy's stocky gut. The air whooshed out of Billy, and he loosened his grip on the rifle. Letting it fall without a second thought, Billy swung a fist at James' face.

He didn't duck in time and took a blow to the temple. Oh that would leave a shiner in the morning. Before he could shake the stars out of his head, Billy delivered another blow to James, who blocked it with his shoulder.

"You think you can come train wiv us? You think you can march wiv us? You're a bloody coward."

Around them, the men and boys chanted about a fight. "Give it to 'im good, Billy!" one man shouted.

And he did. With a swiftness James didn't know Billy possessed, the larger man knocked James to the wooden floor. He landed hard, amid the cheers of the other men. Before he could rise, Billy had dropped a hard knee to his chest.

With his good hand, he grabbed James' Silver War Badge. "You don't deserve this. You couldn't even enlist." With that, he tore it off James' lapel, the fabric tearing under the force.

They chased him off, and James let them. He knew when he was beaten. As he retreated out of the Community Hall, Billy's mocking voice followed him out. "Only a coward would be afraid of a dummy rifle!"

The men's laughter followed him all the way up High Street.

A dummy rifle. Of course. The VTC had no weapons of their own except for training on the rifle range. Even then, it was farmers' own rifles, those who owned them. No man in his right mind would bring a loaded weapon into town.

How stupid was he? His own fear had robbed him of his wits. His desire to redeem himself had ended in disaster. His head ached; his heart ached. His feet yearned to run, but that would destroy the shreds of his dignity. He was a Cowper, a name once respected in Stoweham.

He'd lost his hat back at the Community Hall as well as his last ounce of self-respect. He had nothing to pull down low over his face. His eye must be sporting a real beaut of a shiner by now. Clouds gathered, blocking the late afternoon sun. A chill settled upon his shoulders. As he hastened his way out of town, he did his best to avoid the villagers.

But not all of them avoided him. A bold young chit of a girl, her head almost up to his eyes, but her hair still in pigtails, ran past him, tucking a single white feather into the tear in his lapel. Before he could protest, she dashed off, to the cheers of her friends along the periphery.

So he was nothing more than the village fool now. Even children mocked him. There was no dignity left.

James Cowper ran.

****

James approached the rear of Stoweham House with care. Stoweham House, once the country seat for the noble Cowper family, was all fine porticos and Ionic columns: tall, noble and proud.

He felt unworthy to enter through the grandeur of its neoclassical front door. He'd had it with humanity and humanity had had it with him. His feet ached from running, his shoulder ached from Billy's blows and now it looked like rain. Perfect. Maybe a nice, cold downpour would freeze his aching heart. Hot tears filled his eyes, to burn down his cold cheeks.

No. Only one thing would end this pain.

He slunk past the empty kitchen into the scullery. Here it was dark, warm and dry, and blessedly abandoned. He'd missed tea. No matter. Food was irrelevant now. He searched about until he found the sharpest knife hidden in a drawer. Perfect. He'd considered a rope, but he doubted its efficacy. Poison was a woman's way. But a knife was quick. A knife was sure.

As silently as he entered, James quit the house, to slip off into the bottom garden. The clouds had thickened, and a few spatters of raindrops pricked on his cheeks. He didn't care. Soon it would be all over.

The grounds of Stoweham House backed onto the rear of St. Mary's cemetery. Here, in the older part of the grounds, overgrown with bushes and long grass, tombs of forgotten families dotted the grounds. He and his older sister Joan had wandered through here as children. Later it was him and the village boys, each hoping to catch a glimpse of the Stoweham Ghost or any other specter that might have lurked here.

With rain and suppertime coming on, the cemetery was guaranteed deserted.

He selected the nearest crypt, a low, square, and rather plain little structure, no higher than a kitchen table. The iron door had long been given over to rust and any inscription on the top had weathered away. Who knew what forgotten person lay within?

It was on this final resting place he sat. From there he could not see Stoweham House and only the bell tower of St. Mary's was visible over the tops of trees. No one would find him until morning.

He removed his sack coat and loosened the collar of his shirt. He tested the edge of the knife by brushing over it with his thumb. The honed edge caught on the ridges of his fingerprint. Would it be sharp enough?

Perhaps he should have fetched his razor. No, that would have meant going upstairs. The longer he spent in the house, the greater the chance of running into someone. He did not want to see another human being for as long as he lived. That was another five minutes.

"You can do this," James told himself. He took a few breaths to call upon whatever courage he had left. His hand was as steady as it had ever been, without a shake or tremble. Of course he could do this. He lifted the knife to his throat. One sharp slice, straight down along the vein, should do it. "Goodbye," he told the world.

A gray and white figure rose up out of the tomb. Her hand reached for the knife but passed straight through it and through him.

"Please don't do this," she begged. "I would be terribly sad if you did."

The appearance of a ghost—for that was the only thing she could be—startled James so much he dropped his knife. He scrambled back along the crypt. His hand slipped in the dampness as he nearly fell off.

Still, she proceeded toward him, her hands outstretched.

Oh, good Lord, she was naked. Her generous bosoms were quite on display, their tips pointing straight to him. He dropped his eyes, but the lower sight of her gently-swelling hips and slim legs did not help matters. Instead, he raised his eyes heavenwards. She looked solid enough, as if she was real. She couldn't be real. His mind, having lost its last connection to sanity, was imagining her.

"Please, James…"

She knew his name? Of course she would, if she was a figment of his imagination.

His dour plans forgotten, he tumbled off the crypt, staggered through the long grass, and high-tailed it for home. When he glanced back, he saw her following him, gliding along as if on ice. Yes, definitely naked, without so much as a fig leaf to hide her shame.

The rain came on with greater enthusiasm, splashing his skin and dampening his clothes. His coat he'd left back in the cemetery. No way was he going back for it tonight. The rain fell straight through her. Her curly hair remained unaffected by the moisture, and her pale skin showed no dampness.

He made it through the gate and didn't look back until he'd reached the back door of Stoweham House.

Finally, he was safe inside the house. He shook the images of the naked ghost from his head and plunked down into a kitchen chair. Cook must have retired for the night, having tidied the kitchen and banked the stove. The maid was nowhere to be seen. Thank goodness for small miracles. He wiped the rainwater out of his hair. A single uncovered light bulb provided a wan light. Rain pattered against the window and drummed on the roof. His heart quieted down.

That didn't go to plan at all. He scrubbed his face with his hands and looked heavenward. Surely this was what madness felt like. As he looked about the dim kitchen, a sense of overwhelming loneliness swept over him. Was he to have no succour? Even Death, that specter who claimed all men in the end, refused to have him.

Was there no one who cared about James Cowper?

The ghost floated through the wall and into the kitchen. "I'm sorry, James. But you had to be stopped."

His jaw dropped as he stared at her. She looked far more ethereal this time, less solid. Perhaps it had been the twilight in the cemetery that made her look real. Still, those breasts insisted on staring back at him.

She said, "You're too important to die." She appeared faint, translucent, but her voice was solid.

He shook his head. "You…You're real."

She nodded. "Very much so."

He gestured at her, his hand trembling. "But you're…you're…"

A flash of lightning made them look up to the kitchen window. A crack of thunder, like gunshot, rattled the panes. Spots appeared before James' eyes. He gave in to the darkness and sank to the ground in a faint.

The last thing he heard were the words, "Well, that's useless."

****

James' consciousness gathered itself together from the woolly corners of his mind. He drew a deep breath and opened his eyes. Rain no longer pattered at the window. As he sat up from the flagstone floor, the only sound he heard was the ticking of the kitchen clock.

"I wish you wouldn't do that."

The feminine voice startled him. He leapt back.

There, on the table without a stitch of clothing, sat the ghost. She was faded and white, yet not so wispy he could not see her in the stark electric light of the kitchen's single bulb.

She watched him steadily, unashamed.

He averted his eyes, shading them with his hand. "Did you know you're…"

"A ghost?" came her bright voice.

"Naked." He risked a peek.

She looked down at herself. "Ah, that. Not much I can do about it, I'm afraid. Not much I can do about being a ghost, either." She folded her arms over her bosom and crossed her legs. "Is this better?"

He carefully looked up. "A little. Would you like a robe or something?"

She shook her head. "Won't do me any good. I can't touch anything solid. Believe me, I've tried."

He knew her, now that he had a chance to look at her without embarrassment or the rushing of blood away from his head. "You're the Stoweham Ghost."

She smiled. "I am."

She was also the woman he'd dreamed of since his adolescence. Not true, solid dreams, but rather catching a glimpse of her just before he awakened. Not that he ever saw her when he was fully conscious. "Have you been haunting me?"

Her gaze slid sideways. "I wouldn't call it haunting. But yes. Then again, I haunt everyone who comes to Stoweham House."

James' head spun. He had to sit down. He eased a chair on the far side of the table and fell into it, letting his head fall into his hands. "Why me?"

She smiled and scooted closer. He scooted back, averting his eyes from her bouncing bosoms. As a young man, he'd dreamed about reaching out and caressing those bosoms. Now his shame flooded back to him.

"Because," she said, "I like you."

That only made it worse. Nobody liked him. First, he was the man who wouldn't go off to war, and then he was the man who'd survived. Not everyone who went off to war came back. Those who did come home had left a part of their soul behind. He could see it in their lost little eyes, a nervous glancing to and fro, perhaps in the hopes that if they looked quickly enough, they might catch a glimpse of that sliver of soul that might have followed them home.

They never found it.

He looked up. Her eyes didn't look lost. Instead, he saw a desperation mixed with an optimistic hope. "If you've been haunting me these last few years, why haven't you spoken to me until now?"

She sighed. "Embarrassment. It's not like I'm dressed for company. Besides, you would not have listened to me."

James found that hard to believe. If a ghost, especially a naked ghost, had come up to him and said hello, he would definitely have paid attention. Parts of him were paying attention now. He took a deep breath and imagined a cold bath. "I'm listening now."

Her smile brightened. He didn't think that was possible.

"As everyone else I know is dead, I will have to introduce myself. I am the Honorable Miss Georgia Palmerton, debutante."

James' heart thumped. "You said everyone else. Are there other ghosts I must worry about?" His gaze darted from corner to dark corner of the kitchen, in case more naked ghosts made their appearances.

The Honorable Miss Georgia Palmerton's smile faded. "No. I have seen no other ghosts. As far as I know, I am the only one." She lifted a bare shoulder in a Gallic shrug. "At least, not that I've seen. I don't get about much."

That's not what he had heard, if she was the Stoweham Ghost.

She was famous, this naked lady who roamed about Stoweham and St. Mary's cathedral. There had been a few legends of her showing up during Sunday services and making a bit of a nuisance of herself until the parish priest chased her away.

Georgia Palmerton. He'd never seen the name Palmerton on any of the tombstones in St. Mary's, or on the town register. How did she come to haunt Stoweham? "Do you—did you have family around here?"

She wilted. "No. I haven't seen them in a hundred years. They did come out when I disappeared, in hopes of finding me…" Her brow furrowed in thought. "I was so naïve then. I never approached the only people who would have listened to me and could have helped me because I was too ashamed of my nakedness." She unfolded her arms and looked down at her ever-perky bosoms. "Thus I am trapped here, all because of some silly notion of propriety."

James, discomfited over her unclad form, leapt to his feet. "I need a drink."

Miss Palmerton remained seated on the table while he rummaged about the pantry for cooking sherry. "That's all well and good if you like that horrid stuff. But if you intend on doing some serious drinking, Cook has a bottle of quality stashed behind the runner board under the stove."

James stopped, his hand on the cupboard door. "She does?" His gaze strayed to the boiler stove. "Why would she hide it?"

Miss Palmerton swung her legs. "Because she doesn't use it for cooking."

James fell to his hands and knees, being careful of the hot boiler stove. Sure enough, a section of runner board was loose. There he found a bottle of fine Irish single malt whiskey, mostly full. He planned on putting a serious dent in its quantity.

While he tipped whiskey into a glass, Miss Palmerton settled into the chair opposite.

"You were going to kill yourself."

His glass paused, half-way to his lips. "I beg your pardon?"

"You came to the churchyard, sat on a forgotten tomb, and put a knife to your throat. Your intention was pretty clear."

He downed the glass of whiskey and poured himself another. This one he sipped, as his throat still stung from the first gulp. "That is none of your business."

"It is very much my business. If you kill yourself, who will I talk to?"

"Someone else." Anyone else. He finished the second glass and poured a third. The alcohol burned in his stomach. Maybe it would burn away some of the fear that nagged his heart.

How typical of himself, too afraid to go to war, too afraid to face the villagers, too afraid to even kill himself, even though the world looked like it would be better without him.

She reached out and laid a ghostly hand over his. Her hand sank into his fingers. He shuddered and pulled away, even though he felt nothing.

"Nobody will talk with me," she confessed. "This is the longest conversation I've had in a hundred years."

His vision wavered. As James peered at her, he could see a faint outline of the back of the chair behind her. "Surely someone would have spoken with you." It's not as if the house had been unoccupied all this time. And what about the church? The Ghost of Stoweham wasn't exactly a secret. Many people claimed to have seen her.

She shook her head. "No. Though part of that might be my fault."

She refolded her arms over her bosom, much to James' relief. It was one thing to be stirred by such an image, quite another to be unable to do anything about it, especially if a ghost was around to witness that.

An awkward thought occurred to him; had she watched him get changed? Did she watch him bathe? He consumed a third glass of whiskey to wash away the thought of her voyeurism.

"Nobody wishes to speak with an unclad ghost. This assumes I have the courage to approach them."

She was definitely wavering, as was the whole kitchen. James stared at the bottle of whiskey, now half-empty. No wonder Cook hid this. It was good stuff. "Aren't ghosts supposed to wear sheets or rattle chains or something?"

"I don't know. How many ghosts do you know?"

Good point.

"Anyhow," she continued, "whenever I approach someone, they either recoil in fear and run away, or harass me. Whenever we get a new priest or vicar, I try to speak with them. But that does no good. They either avoid me entirely because of my lack of appropriate clothes, or they try to exorcise me. It's overly rude and never works."

Did the kitchen feel warm? His head felt too heavy for his neck. Also, the humidity pressed close about him. He was just going to lay his head down here on the nice, cool table.

"I intend no harm. I simply need someone to help me," she said.

Sure, thought James as his head buzzed. Perhaps he shouldn't have had so much whiskey. "No problem," he muttered despite his heavy tongue. He pushed the bottle toward her. "Help yourself."

Let the blessed darkness of unconsciousness claim him. It was the only place one could find peace.

Chapter 2
Miss Palmerton's Story

A loud noise rumbling through his splitting headache brought James to consciousness. His mouth tasted terrible, and his heart beat too loudly. He blinked and gently raised his sticky head from the table. The first thing he saw was the ghost sitting next to him, her gaze directed to the other side of the room.

She lifted a transparent finger to her lips and said, "Shhh…"

A startled scream sent crackling waves of pain shooting through his skull. He rose and turned to chastise the screamer. All he saw was the retreating form of the kitchen maid as she slammed the door behind her. At least she took her hysterics someplace else. When he looked back to the table, the ghost had disappeared.

Miss Georgia Palmerton, that was her name. It took him a moment and a sight of the half-empty bottle of whiskey to assure him the Stoweham Ghost was very much real.

So was his headache. A deep drink from the sink and a bit of headache powder from the scullery helped somewhat. He needed a bath and something more comfortable than a kitchen table on which to sleep.

As he made his way upstairs, Miss Palmerton appeared next to him. "May I ask you a favor?"

Before he could answer, noises from above made Miss Palmerton jump. She retreated through the stone wall as the maid-of-all-work came rushing down. She bobbed her head in respect as she dashed past but didn't pause for a word. Best reaction he'd had from anyone in a week.

James made it all the way to his bedroom without seeing another soul. He had no valet or any kind of personal servant, so did not worry that he would be disturbed in his bedroom.

He jumped when Miss Palmerton strode through the wall. "I wish you wouldn't do that," he said, his hand over his thumping heart. The last thing he needed was a fear of young women entering the room, especially by such a phantasmagorical method.

"It's not like I can open the door."

She sat on his bed. Or rather, she appeared to sit. The bed did not sag or sink under her presence.

James retreated to the fireplace mantel and loosened his tie. "I don't think this is entirely proper."

Miss Palmerton looked about. "What? Me in your bedroom? It's not like I haven't been here before."

He shaded his eyes in embarrassment. "I wish you wouldn't remind me." Until today, he'd dismissed those fleeting glimpses to his imagination. With growing dismay, he realized she'd been watching him for a few years now. How many times had he woken to her image after rather lustful dreams? Naturally, she'd fled as soon as he'd awoken, but had she remained, hidden by a curtain? The thought of her witnessing his reaction made him blush. "A young maiden in a man's bedroom isn't proper."

She leaned forward, her arms pressing those lovely

little bosoms up. "Because?"

Did he have to spell it out for her? "What about your reputation?"

Her eyebrow lifted.

"Or mine," he hastily added. He looked over to the window. The curtains were open. He closed them with a jerk. "If anyone sees me here with someone in your state of…" He fluttered his hand up and down as failed to find a proper word.

She rolled her eyes. "No one saw me come in. No one will see me leave. No one is going to notice or care that you are keeping company with the Stoweham Ghost." A transparent hand fluttered over her bosom. "As for my reputation, you will find it impossible to sully."

She rose and floated over to him. He backed up as she approached.

"Go on," she purred. "I dare you to embrace me."

James did his best to keep his gaze above shoulder height. "Why are you tempting me?" The throbbing of his headache resumed.

"I'm not," she replied, pressing closer. She lifted her arms as if to drape them about his shoulders…

And they fell straight through his body.

He felt nothing, though the thought of her passing through him made his skin prickle.

She came forward and passed through him completely. He whirled around to see her exit him and perambulate about the room. Did her perfect bottom have to sway so elegantly as she walked? He shook those distracting thoughts from his head.

"You see," she said. "I cannot interact with the mortal realm. Therefore, you cannot press your advantage and 'ruin me', as they would say." She sighed as she settled back to the bed. It did not shift in response to her presence. "Shame, really. I've always found the Cowper men to be rather handsome." She looked away and sighed in a maidenly fashion.

Handsome? Nobody had ever called him handsome, except Mother. But all mothers said that about their sons. His gaze flickered to the mirror above the mantelpiece. He'd never thought to consider whether he was handsome. Certainly not this morning. His wavy blond hair was askew, his hazel eyes grainy, and his mouth unpleasantly sticky. And his finely tailored gray sack coat had been left in the cemetery.

Sometimes the village girls would press their hands to their lips in shyness and cast coy glances his way when he was a lad, but that had stopped when the Great War came upon them. Then their lips turned up in sneers, and their hands slipped white feathers into his lapel. No. He was not handsome enough to dissuade their scorn.

He definitely needed a bath. "I need you to excuse me while I attend to some important business." He plucked at his waistcoat and shirt, both looking limp and worse for wear.

Miss Palmerton sat up. "Oh, of course." She fiddled with her fingers. "I'll wait for you here."

"Why?"

She looked him straight in the eye. "Because I need your help."

Help, she said. While James scrubbed away the evidence of last night, he pondered on what kind of help a ghost needed. He gave his chin a clean shave and combed his damp hair into place, not that it would stay that way. Wavy hair never did. He didn't spend one second more than necessary looking in the mirror. Neat and clean he was, nothing more. Certainly not handsome.

The door knob rattled, startling him. His heart thumped. Was it the ghost?

No. She would have simply walked through the walls. Even so, she had promised to stay hidden in the bedroom. Still, he was glad he'd locked the door.

"James?" called Mother's voice. "Is that you in there?"

Ah, it was the living. "Yes. Nearly finished, Mum."

"Do be quick. There's a bit of an issue with one of the servants. I simply can't face it until I am at my best."

James sighed. Ever since Father died, Mother had been unable to cope with the running of Stoweham House. The number of servants dwindled to half and many of the rooms were shut up. Even with his aunt living there, Stoweham House became harder and harder each year to maintain. James would groan as he watched the family fortune dwindle. The Great War didn't help matters any, nor did his reputation for cowardice.

He finished his ablutions, put the cap back on the tooth powder, and surrendered the bathroom to Mother.

Miss Palmerton waited for him in the bedroom, studying a small picture of a boy and dog hanging on his wall.

Why did his eyes have to look at her perfectly round little bottom? He redirected his gaze.

She looked over her shoulder and gave him a beautiful smile. "Feel better?"

"Somewhat." He plucked at his dressing gown. He'd removed his dirty clothes prior to his bath but had forgotten to bring clean clothing with him.

She gestured to the painting. "Did you know this portrait was of your great-great uncle when he was a boy? The dog wasn't his but belonged to one of the outside servants. Poor lad. Dogs made him sneeze. He was terribly upset that he was the only boy he knew who didn't have a dog. So he refused to sit for the portrait unless he was painted with a dog." She sighed. "Charlotte gave in, in the end. She always did."

He pulled a shirt out of the wardrobe. "Could I have a moment of privacy, please? I need to change."

"Go right ahead," Miss Palmerton replied. "I promise I won't look."

He blushed. "I'd prefer it if you were out of the room entirely."

That got her attention. She turned around. He clutched the shirt to his chest and couldn't meet her gaze. "It's awkward with you here. I'm not used to changing before an audience."

"How very missish of you," she replied.

However, she did depart the room and gave him a few blessed minutes of privacy. With his gray suit in such a mess, he settled for his old green suit. Not the best of fashion, but at least it was clean.

She returned as he was lacing up his shoes. "There's quite a to-do downstairs. The kitchen maid is threatening to quit, and Cook is most upset someone found her good whiskey."

James' hands paused over his laces. How long would it be before the domestic chaos landed in his lap? Hiding upstairs for the next couple of hours sounded like a very good idea. Any attempt to sneak out could result in disaster.

As he was trapped for the nonce, James settled onto his bed, his back against the headboard. He looked at the painting on the wall. It had hung there as long as he could remember. Did he know who the little boy was? Had ever bothered to ask? Or care?

Miss Palmerton settled nearby.

"How long have you been a ghost?" he asked.

She huffed a breath while she considered. "Well on a hundred years now, if I count correctly. After a while, time loses its meaning. It gets lonely as the years pass by. I miss the Season." Her face lit up in memory. "Have you ever done a London Season?"

James shook his head. By the time he was old enough, the Great War had come and the Season as a social event declined. Even so, he doubted his cousin Reggie would welcome him, Mother, and Aunt Violet to the town house, especially as his son Emory was not yet back from war.

Miss Palmerton spun off the bed. "Oh, a Season in London is splendid!" She danced about the room as if at a ball.

James had to shade his eyes. It would not be proper to observe her deshabille, no matter how much he wanted to.

"I love dancing at the balls." Her form whirled to a stop in front of him. "Do you dance?"

Oh goodness, now he had to look up. Way up. He stood so her bosom was no longer at eye-level. "I did learn a few. My mother insisted."

She bounced in excitement. "Such as?"

"Oh, castle walk, foxtrot, had to learn the waltz—"

She gasped. "The waltz? Did you ever get to dance it in public?"

Had he? Come to think of it, when was the last dance he attended? Must have been at least five years, if not longer. Certainly well before the Great War.

Miss Palmerton didn't wait for his answer. "I learned the basic steps of the waltz, but I was never allowed to dance it in public. I always wanted to." She held out her hand. "Dance with me now?" Her eyes shone with eagerness.

James had reached out his hand before he remembered she was a ghost. "How will we dance? I can't touch you, so how can I lead?"

Her smile wavered before she pushed it back onto her face. "Please." Was that a quiver in her voice? "Just…let us try." She swallowed.

His heart ached for her. How long had it been since she'd had an honest-to-goodness conversation with another living soul, much less danced with one? James stood up. He held out his arms and kept his gaze high.

Miss Palmerton wiped at a corner of her eye and moved into his embrace, laying a ghostly hand over his raised one and settling the other on his shoulder. "Now what?"

He racked his brains. "Triple-time," he suggested. How did the steps go? Forward, side, side? "One, two, three. One, two, three." He moved forward, straight through her then froze, afraid he might have hurt her.

Miss Palmerton squeaked and backed up. "I beg your pardon. I'll do my best to keep up."

James needed a moment to catch his breath. While he couldn't feel her, the thought of her going through him was disconcerting. It wasn't that it was frightening, but the thought of them being together deeper than skin was rather intimate. His hands shook, but he kept them up. "If you watch my eyes, you'll be able to follow."

Miss Palmerton nodded.

"Ready? One, two, three…" He stepped forward and she stepped back. But when he stepped to the side, she didn't step far enough and his arm went through her head.

"Oh dear," she declared and took a half-step to catch up. "It's so hard when I can't feel you. Perhaps I should watch your feet instead?"

He certainly couldn't watch hers. "If it makes it easier." He raised his arms for dancing. "One, two, three…"

With Miss Palmerton watching his feet, they danced the first few steps of the waltz.

"When I learned it," she said, her focus on his feet unwavering, "I learned it 'long, short, short'. A shame I never got to dance it in public."

James guided her through a few more figures before she gave up, stopping short. He slid through her and came to a halt. "What's wrong?" His arms fell to the side.

Looking at him with sad eyes, she placed a hand over his arm. Her fingers dipped in and out of the fabric of his sleeve. "I realized why it was considered scandalous if danced without approval." She drew back to her dance position close to his chest. "You stand so close you can't help but gaze into each other's eyes. You communicate not by words but by subtle movements." She raised up on tiptoe to whisper in his ear. "And secrets can be shared with no one the wiser." Slowly, she withdrew to the other side of the room.

"Thank you for dancing with me."

"My pleasure." He sat on the bed. "Why weren't you permitted to dance? Did your parents think it too fast?"

Her gloominess evaporated as a smile crossed her face. "Oh no. All debutantes were forbidden, of course. Only matrons may dance the waltz, if given permission. One's deportment must be impeccable."

"If debutantes weren't permitted, why did you learn?"

Miss Palmerton sat on the opposite side of the bed from him, a coy smile on her lips. "I would not always be a debutante." A flicker of sorrow creased her forehead before she pushed it away.

James inspected his hands. "I hope I am not too forward in asking if you had any prospects." This was awkward. "I mean, it sounds like you had, um, someone? That is…"

She reached across the bed and patted his hand. "It's all right. I've come to terms with what happened.

"Yes, I had someone, or rather, I was about to: a beau of impeccable character and good family, Lord Auberon Cowper."

James drew in a breath. "Cowper? One of my ancestors?"

"Yes." She counted on her fingers. "Your great-great-great…" she paused, "grandfather, I think. I'd have to consult Debrett's. Anyhow, mine is a bittersweet tale, but rest assured your ancestor conducted himself admirably, especially in the face of my loss."

"I'm sorry." He studied this young woman. How difficult it was to think she could have been his great-

great-something-great grandmother. She didn't look a day over twenty-one. He couldn't pin a hundred years of age and experience to this fresh face and lithe body. "What happened?"

Miss Palmerton closed her eyes and drew a century-old memory from her depths. "It was the end of the Season and the hot days of summer. Lord Auberon had invited many of us for a week of sport and games here at his country residence. Now, His Lordship and I had often kept company during the Season, and I knew he had a fondness for me. Indeed, even though he had not spoken in exact terms, we did have an understanding. I fully expected a forthcoming proposal." Her fingers traced the pattern on the bedspread. "Nobody knew of his intentions. Indeed, on my part, I only suspected."

James sighed. Had the poor maiden gotten her hopes up only to have them dashed? "Did he propose?"

"We never got that far. Lord Auberon was quite the catch, and many an eligible young lady set her cap for him. One particular lady by the name of Miss Charlotte Capel expressed a strong interest in him. Because her father and Lord Auberon's late father were political chums, she had been invited along to the party. I don't know what sort of promises she thought she'd been given, but she made quite the cake of herself for the sake of Lord Auberon. And jealous. You'd never seen such green eyes. In front of Lord Auberon, she was all simpers and giggles. But when it was just us ladies, she made it well and truly known that she would brook no competition." Miss Palmerton shook her head. "In reality, she never had a chance."

James watched her hands move over the bed. He

wanted to take it and hold it and never let go. "But you didn't have a promise either. I mean, nothing had been declared."

Satisfaction smoothed out her face. "I had declaration enough. Two days before the party was to have ended, Lord Auberon and I slipped outside during a card party. There, under the stars and surrounded by the scent of freesia, he leaned over and gave me the most beautiful kiss any lady could ever want." She closed her eyes and pressed her fingers to her lips.

James envied Miss Palmerton her memory. How lovely it must be to know one was cherished. His heart ached. He'd fancied a few girls in the past, but none of them had returned his affections. Nothing kills young love like a cold shoulder. His recent reputation for cowardice had all but killed any possibility of romance.

Miss Palmerton opened her eyes. "And that is how she found us."

James sighed. Miss Palmerton was caught kissing Lord Auberon by a jealous rival?

But she had a soft, dreamy smile on her face. "At least one of my last memories was one of bliss." She closed her eyes and flopped back on the bed, nearly sinking half-way through it. "Oh, I miss dancing and kissing and holding hands and the scent of flowers and eating good food." She laid a hand over her tummy. "Sometimes I imagine my stomach growling."

James put a hand on his own. It felt pretty empty. "At least, a dead person doesn't have to worry about eating."

Miss Palmerton sat up. "Oh, but I'm not dead."

He blinked at her. "I'm pretty sure you are."

"No, I'm not."

James did something bold. He swiped his hand through her midsection. "You're clearly a ghost. Live people have bodies."

She smiled at him. "I do have a body. I'm only separated from it, that's all."

"That's what death is."

"But I know where my body is." She said it as if it was a pair of comfortable shoes or the hat she wore last Sunday.

"Where is it?" James looked about with concern. Surely a corpse wasn't resident in the cellar or the attic or worse—in the walls or under the floorboards. Sleeping with a ghost in the house was one thing, even a ghost who watched him, but sleeping with a dead body nearby? Entirely different matter.

"In St. Mary's graveyard."

His anxiety fled, leaving nothing but blessed relief. "Of course it is. That's where dead bodies go."

She leaned over. "If I'm dead, then why hasn't my body rotted away?"

He withdrew from her. "It…what?"

"It's as hale and whole as the day…" Her brow furrowed. She caught her lower lip between her teeth. "It's still there as it's been for the past hundred years. That's why I say I'm not dead. However, I'm not exactly alive, am I?" She turned from him. "A hundred years and I never thought that I wasn't alive." She looked at her hands. "I mean, I can see myself, as can you. I can reason, I have my own thoughts. It's as if I was living, only I'm not."

"I'm sorry." It was the only thing he could think to say that wasn't trite or dismissive. But one thing was certain. Dead was dead. The sooner she accepted it, the better it would be. "How did you die?"

Her eyes flickered up at him. "I don't think 'death' is the best word, but until I find another, it will do. It was Miss Capel and a spell gone wrong."

"What? A magic spell?"

"What other kind of spells are there?" Miss Palmerton scooted to the headboard and stared at her hand.

Fair enough. If he could be sitting on his bed talking to a ghost, then why not magic spells?

She stopped studying her hand and floated over to James. "Don't tell me you've never come across magic before."

He shook his head.

"What? Never? What about your mother's charms? Household protections? Anti-loss enchantments?"

He denied knowledge of any of it.

She floated back to the headboard, surprised. "How odd. No wonder you've had such terrible luck."

He opened his mouth to protest before reconsidering. He'd had a bad run of it ever since the Great War began, with things getting worse every year. Surely it didn't mean magic at play, did it? Or lack thereof? "So what happened to you?"

"The next day Miss Capel lured me to the back of the garden with an anonymous note and a promise of a gift for me from 'you know who'. I thought it might have been Lord Auberon finally proposing. What else was I to think when I find a beautiful box with a ring inside? I did what any other young lady would have done. I put it on." She shuddered. "I don't know where she got it. Surely she didn't make it herself, because it takes a long time to imbue an item with magic. Maybe a gypsy woman? Anyhow the moment I put on the ring, I fell down as if dead."

Dead. He knew it.

Her fingers traced the bedspread again. "After my body dropped to the ground, Miss Capel came out from hiding. That's how I knew it was her. She gloated about how I'd stay out of her way for the rest of the party and so on. After a while, she stopped and really looked at me. I wasn't moving. She nudged at me, then rolled me on to my back and listened for breath. I had none. That frightened her. It frightened me too, for I was standing there, watching her and myself. It was very disconcerting. I said, 'What have you done?' That's when she looked up at me and screamed. It was supposed to be a sleeping spell, she confessed, designed to make me sleep the next few days away. It wasn't supposed to kill me."

"So you are dead." James knew it.

She held up a finger. "I'm getting to that part. Granted, that is what we both thought in the beginning. I begged her to go get help, but she refused. If anyone found out what she'd done, her reputation would have been ruined forever. So she did what any guilty party would have done—hid the evidence. Knowing that my absence would be noted, she knew she had to hide my body where no one would think to look, St. Mary's graveyard. There she found an old crypt with a loose door. It was in here she secreted my body, closed the door, and ran away." She grew quiet. Her hand poked at the bedspread, her actions getting sharper and sharper until her fingers slid through the cover. "I sat there until midnight, shocked at what had happened to me. It wasn't until much later that I realized that I needed to do something about this. So I fled to Stoweham House in hopes of attracting attention." She grimaced. "Oh, I attracted attention, all right. I arrived after the ladies had withdrawn for the night, but the men were still at their brandy. I dashed into the dining room and cried for help."

James had this flash of vision of Miss Palmerton running naked through the house. That would not have gone down well with the guests. "Did anyone listen?"

She shook her head. "They were too far gone in their cups to realize what I had become. A few of them made lewd suggestions, including comments on my…" She gestured with her hands at her bosoms. "That's when I realized I was naked. Oh, the shame! As soon as I recognized my state, I fled. A young lady simply isn't seen unclothed, even when she is dead."

Now James sat up. "There, you said it. Dead."

Miss Palmerton inclined her head. "Indeed, that is what I believed at the time. I was here, and my body somewhere else. Like you said, that is the definition of dead." She waved her hand dismissively. "I won't bore you with the details of my going missing and everyone's grief."

"And you didn't bother to talk to anyone the way you are talking to me now?"

Miss Palmerton stood up, or rather, she brought herself upright, with her legs disconcertingly stuck into the bed and her very bare torso suspended above it. She spread her arms so nothing was hidden. "I have no clothes in this form. I was quite embarrassed. I hid myself away and watched as they searched for me. My family was notified; they came, and still I was too ashamed to show myself. In the face of such tragedy, everyone quit Stoweham House. Lord Auberon locked it up in his grief, even taking away the skeleton staff, leaving me alone." She pulled herself out of the bed and settled back to the headboard in an imitation of normalcy. "I could go as far as St. Mary's. When the loneliness got too much, I sought out the parish priest. A man of the cloth should know about death and could possibly help me. However, I was still ashamed of my nakedness and had trouble approaching him." She lifted a shoulder in a forlorn gesture. "He, however, had no interest in listening to ghosts. Every time I attempted to speak to him, he attempted to exorcise me. Wouldn't listen to a word I said. Also, the exorcisms never worked."

James said, "So the legend of the Stoweham Ghost was born?"

She nodded. "Took me years to get over my prudishness. By the time I was brave enough to approach someone, Victoria's morality had sunk in and nobody was willing to speak to me. Terribly improper, they believed."

He ran a hand over his newly-shaven face, his fingers gingerly going over a sore spot on his jaw. No doubt a bruise would manifest itself in a day or two. "So you didn't speak to anyone in, what? Twenty years?"

"Not casually, no." Her countenance darkened. She crawled closer. "However, when I was angry enough, I didn't care what I looked like. Three years," she growled. "I spent three years staring at an empty house and hiding from St. Mary's parishioners. Three long, lonely years, until Stoweham House was opened once more. Lord Auberon returned. This time he brought a wife and a baby." She shook her head in disappointment.

"Was it Miss Capel?" James ventured.

Miss Palmerton nodded.

"I'm sorry."

She looked away. "Well, what can one do?"

"It must have been unbearable."

She agreed. "I was so angry. That could have been me." She sighed and sank down to the bed. "I confess I behaved badly. I confronted her one night. Scared the living daylights out of her, I did. She fled to the other side of the house and refused to go back into that room ever again."

"And you didn't pursue her?"

She didn't answer at first. James reached out his hand, but hesitated. How did one comfort a ghost?

"I did," she confessed finally. "As she ran, I followed. But I discovered something unpleasant. The further I move from my body, the fainter I become."

Only then did James have a good, honest look at Miss Palmerton. He'd not directly looked at her since first encountering her because of her nakedness. Now that he gave her full consideration, she did look rather transparent, very ghostlike. He thought back to last night when she had appeared in the graveyard. She'd looked solid like a real person. Then, she'd startled him. Then in the kitchen, white and faded, she looked like ghost. Here, even more removed, she was ethereal. Still detectable, but could never have been mistaken for a living being.

She looked in the direction of the rest of the house. "If I go too far…"

"You mean you turn invisible?"

A shudder ran through her form. "No. If I was merely invisible, I would still be there, only unseen. I…" The shudder ran through her again. "If I go too far, I believe I'll disappear completely."

What was she saying? "You mean you've never tried it?"

"I have not had the courage." She slid off the bed and moved to the wall, the one closest to St. Mary's graveyard, all the way on the other side of the property. "When I get to a certain point, I stop feeling my hands and feet. Move further and I start losing sense of my limbs." She drew a breath, more out of mortal habit than need. "I fear if I move too far away, I'll be lost forever."

That was a sobering thought. "Then you'd truly be dead."

She nodded. "And why would I want to pursue death when I might still be alive?" She drifted closer to the bed, closer to James.

He moved to make room for her on the bed.

She accepted his wordless offer and sat next to him. "I spent a few years believing I was dead. One day, when I had summoned the courage, I returned to my corpse. Only it wasn't the moldering bones I was expecting, but as fresh and clean as if I was merely sleeping. That gave me hope. Maybe Miss Capel's spell had only been one of a deep, deep sleep, like the fairy tales. If this was so, then I might still be alive. She wrapped her arms about her. "It comforts me, sometimes, to think I may be alive. When I feel all Friday-faced, I will go spend time with my body to remind me that I still live. And if I live, perhaps hope does as well. I was doing just that when you came and sat on my tomb. And so that's how I found you, when you sat on the crypt, one of the last people I expected attempting the last thing I expected of him. I have told you my tale. Now you must tell me yours. For someone who still inhabits his body, why do you want to kill yourself?"

James' heart froze. Why had she asked that direct question? He swallowed, his throat suddenly dry. "Because I have no good reason to live."

"Pish-tosh," she scoffed. "Surely it's not that bad."

He stared at her, incredulous. "Not that bad? I've been labeled the village coward."

"And are you?"

That left him speechless. It wasn't as if he could blurt out, "Yes." But at the same time he couldn't say, "No." That left only the truth: "Handling a rifle terrifies me."

She nodded. "When was the last time you held a rifle?"

"Yesterday."

"Goodness," she exclaimed. "So this is an everyday event?"

He shook his head. "I was only doing my duty, or trying to." He briefly shared yesterday's Volunteer Corps experience, including his shameful beating and retreat.

"Well," replied Miss Palmerton, "That explains the black eye."

James frowned. "I don't have a black eye."

She reached out transparent fingers to his face. "You do."

"Surely I would have seen it in the mirror this morning." This might have been a lie. He couldn't bear the thought of looking at himself. Even he couldn't bear the sight of a coward.

She snorted. "I'm very surprised you didn't. I advise you look now."

He huffed. Pushing himself off the bed, he departed for the bathroom, now empty of Mother. When he wiped the steam off the glass and peered in, he saw Miss Palmerton was correct. His left eye sported quite the shiner. How could he have missed it? What other injuries had he ignored? He ran a hand over his jaw. It had been sore earlier. Now it throbbed. His shoulder wasn't terribly comfortable either. He lifted an arm and a sharp pain jabbed through his muscles. His back, likewise, when he shifted from side to side, had a certain painful stiffness to it.

A ghostly face appeared over his shoulder in the mirror.

"I told you," Miss Palmerton said.

James jumped. "Could you not do that?"

"*Désolé,*" she apologized. "I must ask, who darkened your daylights? They did a spectacular job."

"Everyone. I told you the village didn't appreciate my apparent cowardice. Nearly beat me to death, they did." He wilted, only the sink keeping him upright.

"So you thought to finish the job?"

The only answer he gave her was a resentful stare.

"Only asking," she said. "They say they don't want you, that you're worthless. Do you agree with them?"

Anger flared in his eyes, and he whirled to face her. "I don't need some ghost with no sense of modesty telling me what I can and can't do!"

She was nonplussed. "You didn't answer my question."

He threw his hands in the air. "I don't need this," he muttered and he left the bathroom.

Miss Palmerton followed. "This is exactly what you need."

"I won't let you interfere." Why couldn't he walk away from her? Oh, wait. He could. She herself had said she couldn't go to the other side of the house. She'd fade away, possibly for good.

James stomped down the staircase. At the bottom he'd retreat to the library. She'd never be able to follow him there.

She trailed after him. "I don't need your permission. I'll interfere as much as I want, and you can't stop me."

She fled with purpose down the stairs, and instead of turning right in the direction of the library, she went left toward the kitchen and, to his dawning horror, the breakfast room. Mother and Aunt Violet were not so posh they insisted on breakfast in bed. Every morning they retreated to the quiet little breakfast room to dine quietly on toast and soft-boiled eggs.

James followed too late. As he burst into the breakfast room, he heard Miss Palmerton's distinctive voice say, "Your son wishes to kill himself. I recommend you have a chat with him first."

She threw a defiant glare at him over her shoulder before she disappeared through the wall.

His gaze fell upon the shocked look on his aunt's face. But that was nothing compared to the sheer sorrow that infused Mother's countenance.

His soul sank inside him. All he'd thought of was his own pain and how the world would have been better without him. He'd not given any thought to the one person who had brought him into the world and had an overwhelming desire that he stay.

Bloody hell.

Chapter 3
James' Story

Several painful hours later, a contrite and tear-stained James Cowper made his way through the grounds of Stoweham House to the wall that separated the far garden from the older part of St. Mary's cemetery. A small gate, forgotten by most people, allowed movement between the two properties.

James approached the low crypt, barely high enough to slide in a few coffins, nothing more. It was plain and square and entirely unobtrusive, an ideal garden bench if one didn't mind hopping up. At one end of the crypt was an iron door, like one would find on a stove, only this one was more rust than iron, probably stuck shut. Not that a ghost would need to open a door.

So here he was. He had told himself he was coming to fetch his gray sack coat and the knife he'd dropped in his startlement.

Miss Palmerton was nowhere to be seen. He looked at the crypt and wondered what it would have been like to have been stuck there for a century, unable to roam more than a quarter mile, if that, from where one reposed.

From behind him, Miss Palmerton said, "You came back?"

He jumped but didn't turn around. "That was a

cruel thing you did."

"I'm not sorry," she replied. "Someone I've watched and lov—known for years decides to die on my crypt and you think I'm going to stand by and do nothing?"

He flipped his hand back toward the house. "My mother is up in her room crying her eyes out. She's been there for hours and may have taken to the bed for a week because of what you did." He refused to look at Miss Palmerton.

"She would have been doing that had you succeeded in what you planned to do. At least this way when she's all cried out, she can hug you and be grateful I stopped you."

"I'd hardly call her grateful."

This ghostly young lady remained behind him, not that he would have heard her if she'd moved.

"That's because she's angry. At you. Not me, you."

"You don't know that," he said, although she was right. Fury had tinged the sorrow that had consumed his mother. He'd spent a good hour trying to reassure her that he would not kill himself. She'd also said a few things that unsettled him, things about him being the end of the line and how he hadn't done anything about it.

He wrinkled his nose. It wasn't like he could do anything about it here in Stoweham. Society had all but shunned him. No woman of any station would give him the time of day, much less engage in a courtship. Whether he died yesterday or died sixty years down the road, it didn't matter, because he didn't have an heir.

Not that the inheritance of his branch of Cowpers were terribly rich or titled. His grandfather, to pay death duties, had sold off most of his property in the eighteen-nineties. The townhouse and the country house he had divided between his two sons. Stoweham House, grand but expensive, was pretty much all that was left of the Cowper holdings in James' possession.

And it came with a rather inconvenient ghost.

"You're jealous," he stated.

Now she swanned into his view. She glided around him until only the crypt lay between them. "Too right I am. Even when—especially when—you don't have a good enough reason for dying."

He spread his arms. "What? The derision of everyone I know isn't enough?"

To her credit, she didn't play the mother card again. Instead, she said, "Then you don't know many people."

This was true. However, in spite of their numbers, none of them held him in any respect. "I know enough."

"Perhaps they don't know you." Her fingers trailed along the crypt before her.

"Do you know what a white feather means?" Very bold young ladies would tuck white feathers into the upper pocket of any man appearing to shirk doing his duty for King and Country. He'd been gifted with so many he could create his own flock of chickens.

She nodded. "I read the papers."

That surprised him. "You do? How?"

She splayed her hands over the crypt. "The kitchen maid covers the table with yesterday's news when she does messy work. I'll read as many articles as I can when she's not there."

"I can't go into Stoweham village without someone throwing a white feather at me." Or rocks, or insults, or punches. "Nobody wants me, nobody respects me."

"Simply because you didn't go to war?" She shook her head. "Lots of men didn't go to war."

He turned away from her. His head wanted his feet to walk away from her, but his feet weren't listening. "It's because I'm a coward. Even if I did go to war, I would never have survived."

She made a disapproving sound. "So you were killing yourself because you didn't die in a war?"

He turned around in time to see her roll her eyes and cross her arms over her bosom. "You don't understand."

"It's war. It never makes sense." Her brow furrowed and she pressed her lips together. "This has nothing to do with the war, does it?" She put her hand to her forehead. "This is something that happened over ten years ago, before you were out of short pants." Miss Palmerton settled onto the top of the crypt, her ankles crossed, her hands folded neatly in her lap, her breasts uncovered. "I remember something happening to you, but I was never able to find out what. You never spoke of it to anyone. Your parents simply thought you were being young. Now that I think of it, what happened to you?"

His heart thumped. Why did she have to be so right? Of course this all led back to one incident. He hadn't told anyone out of fear of getting into trouble. The other boys had said nothing at the time. However, they had never forgotten. It was as if they'd left the secret in their hearts too long, letting it molder until it erupted in poison, driven by the unspoken terror of war.

James took a breath. He intended to take the secret with him to the grave. But wasn't Miss Palmerton already dead? "When I was fourteen, one of the other boys had gotten his father's rifle. We thought it all manly to shoot a rifle. So we headed out to the forest to take potshots at tin cans." He didn't dare close his eyes. The images came back to him as vivid as the day they happened. "Billy grew bored. He thought he'd have some fun, so he snuck up behind me and fired the rifle just over my shoulder." Heat suffused James' cheeks. "I jumped and, like the coward I was, I ran. Billy thought that great sport, so he chased after me, firing the rifle."

He'd run and run, the sound of gunfire and the hoots of laughter from the other boys ringing in his ears. They'd chased him all the way across a paddock into Farmer Granger's barn. There, they'd cornered him, where James wet himself when Billy had fired the rifle into the air one last time.

Billy's last shot was pure folly, for that brought Farmer Granger out.

The boys all ran away, except for James, who was too frightened to move. His father had applied the strop to his young backside when he refused to tell what happened, and even when he refused to give up the names of the boys involved. You didn't grass on your mates.

But they weren't his mates, were they? Ever since that day, the other boys had given him a wide berth. They never stopped by to ask him to play and gave him the cold shoulder. At the time he thought it was worse to be a squealer rather than a coward. By the time he'd realized his error, it was too late. Since then, the sound of a rifle sent him into cold shivers.

"James?" Miss Palmerton asked.

He shook himself out of his distraction. "Sorry."

He looked about. On the far side of the graveyard, a wall separated a farmer's paddock from the churchyard. Beyond that, he could see the trees of the forest. Funny, but he had no problems roaming between the trees.

"Nothing to be sorry about. Is that why you did not go to war?"

He ran a hand over his mouth and nodded. "The Derby Scheme came to town, looking to form a Pals Brigade. I thought if I joined up like everyone else was doing, they'd stop thinking of me as a coward. In the recruitment office they asked if I'd ever handled a gun. I didn't know how to answer them. Then they shoved one in my hands, and I fainted on the spot."

Right in front of the other lads. Despite his effort, every time he attempted to enlist, he'd faint. The doctor declared him unfit for duty, physically incapable. They handed him a Certificate of Exemption. Several years later when young ladies started denuding geese in an effort to shame able-bodied men, the government had issued Silver War Badges.

"So no war for you." Miss Palmerton sighed in pity.

"No war, no honor, no respect." James lifted his fingers to his lapel. During the altercation at the VTC, his pin had been torn from his coat—not that it had protected him from the scorn of the village. Still, it had been his and the government did not issue replacements. "No life, and now no death."

Miss Palmerton had listened to his story, her chin in her hand.

"So there you have it. I tried to do my part. I've been excused from recruitment, but nobody will believe me. I don't know what to do."

At this, she sat up. "You don't? I thought it most obvious."

James blinked at her.

She gave him a broad, sunny smile. "You leave Stoweham."

James' jaw dropped. "I can't leave Stoweham."

"Why not?"

"Because I live here."

"So?"

He ran his hands through his hair, disrupting its neatly-combed appearance. "One does not up sticks and move away from their village."

"It doesn't mean you can't." Her incredulous gaze made his skin prickle.

"It doesn't mean I should."

She threw her arms into the air. "Of course it means you should. It's not like you're trapped here." With those words, the fire left her. She wrapped her arms about her and turned away. "Like me." She bowed her head.

Guilt snagged at his insides with sharp little fingers. He never meant to make her cry. Did ghosts cry? He reached out a hand toward her shuddering shoulder. Even if he could touch her, he didn't dare. "I'm sorry. I didn't know."

All she could do was shake her head. Her curls bounced. He wanted to reach out and touch them.

James withdrew his hand. "I've been a cad." He sank against the crypt. "I've been so wrapped up in my own problems, I failed to realize—"

"Everyone's failed to realize. A hundred years I've been here, hiding my naked self in shame. A hundred years of trying to speak with people. A hundred years of watching generation after generation of Cowpers being birthed, marrying and dying. A century of hiding in the dark corners of St. Mary's, watching parishioners keeping pews warm with their bottoms while their hearts remain as ice. Imagine spending more than a lifetime being judged by how one looks."

He glanced up and down at her figure and form, all lithe limbs and bare skin. Like all the adolescent boys of the village, he'd hoped to get a glimpse of the famed naked Stoweham Ghost. If only he'd known she'd been watching him this whole time. No wonder that this was the longest conversation she'd had in a hundred years. Any lad would have seen nothing but an unclad young lady. Any woman would have given in to her sensibilities and either screamed or fainted at the sight of a ghost, or shunned her entirely out of propriety.

James hopped up onto the crypt next to Miss Palmerton. She almost looked substantial, if faded. "I'm sorry." He drew a breath. "I promise I will listen to you."

Hope dawned in her eyes. "Really?"

He nodded. What did he have to lose? A tiny corner of his soul, one he'd thought had gone for good, stirred at the thought of keeping company with a beautiful young lady whose charms were on full display. Another corner rejoiced that someone was speaking to him without the greasy layer of his cowardly reputation staining their conversation. He wanted to reach out for her hand, but the ethereal nature of her form daunted him somewhat.

Miss Palmerton's face lit up. "Promise you'll listen to me for the next five minutes and not shirk?"

The levity that had lifted his spirits from the nadir

of his soul deflated somewhat. "Why? What are you going to say?"

She shrugged casually and looked away. "Nothing that I haven't tried asking other people."

Ah. One of the legends of the Stoweham Ghost was that she attempted to entice you into the graveyard, presumably to your death. Still, he'd promised to listen. Either way, he could not lose.

She slid off the crypt and knelt by one end. "Already you've listened to me and you have come to my resting place. There is but two things left."

He swallowed, stars dancing before his eyes. He sent up a silent prayer that he would not faint again in front of this ghost. "What do I need to do?"

She beamed at him. "First, I need you to crack open the door to this crypt."

James slid off and knelt beside her. The end of the crypt was blocked by a very rusty iron door. It had fallen off its hinges long ago. Now it lay propped up over the opening, with only a puddle of rust keeping it in place. At the top of the door was the thinnest of gaps. Not quite big enough to get a hand through, but only just big enough to peer inside—not that James had any desire to look there. Besides, he reasoned, it was too dark to see anything.

Hmm. James studied the door. It was more a case of prying it off, rather than swinging it open. A fruitful search of a more neglected corner of the graveyard yielded a stout branch that had fallen from an oak. This he inserted in the gap at the top of the door. He levered and pulled and poked at the door, sending showers of rust onto the weeds below.

Miss Palmerton bounced in eagerness, her bosoms

48

quivering in a most distracting manner.

The branch broke just as the middle of the door gave way in layered sheets of rust. The sides remained stuck to the crypt. Was that something pale inside? James shoved that thought aside as he fetched another, smaller branch. Not thinking about the contents, James focused on prising back the remains of the door.

With a final explosion of rust, the last half of the door came away. There, in stain of rust and decayed linen lay the crumpled form of a body.

Miss Palmerton.

James drew a shuddery breath and backed away from the crypt. Miss Capel had not done a tidy job of hiding her evidence. Miss Palmerton's body had been crammed in the crypt in a most undignified manner. Only her thigh and her back were visible, so folded up she was. Her body, where it rested against the door, was stained with rust. All that remained of her linen afternoon gown was tatters. The dirt inside the crypt had darkened it so much one could not tell the original color. One thing was certain; her body had not decayed away as one would have expected.

No wonder Miss Palmerton had such high hopes.

Her ghost laughed in delight and clapped her silent hands in glee. "Now, let's find that ring."

He hesitated. He wasn't used to needing his courage so much. Indeed, he'd been calling on it rather a lot lately; surely it had grown weary of his demands.

Still, he had promised he'd help. He crouched down and reached out a hand. It hesitated over her flesh.

"It's all right," Miss Palmerton reassured him. "You can touch me."

He did, laying a hand on her back. He jerked it back as fast as he could. "You're cold!" He had been half-expecting her body to be warm, if it was still alive.

Miss Palmerton's ghost crouched down beside him and stuck her head inside. "Am I? I guess that's what happens when one lives in a crypt."

James shook the chill from his hand and rocked back to sit on the long grass. Seeing her pop in and out of solid objects made his courage waver. "Could you please not do that?"

She pulled back. "I apologize." She settled next to him, more into the grass than onto it. "I'm so used to curling up within myself. Sometimes I was trying to put myself back together, other times, simply resting next to someone who wasn't afraid of my company."

A cold thought occurred to him. "Are you the only body in that crypt?"

"Technically? No, though the other two occupants—"

"Two occupants?" How many dead bodies were in there?

"—are nothing more than a few bones and splinters of wood. They've been dead even longer than I have."

Nervousness made his hand tremble. It was one thing to see Miss Palmerton's body there, but the thought he might touch a skeleton made his skin crawl all over. He closed his eyes. No way he could do this.

"Please," she murmured close into his ear. "Please don't give up now. We're so close."

His heart thumped, and he opened his eyes. Everyone in the village thought him a coward. They laughed at him that day in the barn, and they'd sneered at him when he'd fainted in front of the recruiters. They mocked him and drove him away from the village despite his Certificate of Exemption and, later, his Silver War Badge. That had been torn off during the scuffle at the Volunteer Training Corps.

Everyone thought him a coward, and he let himself believe it.

If any one of them were here, in his place, having prised open a crypt on holy ground, would any of them have the stomach to pull out a body? The more he thought on it, the more he knew they didn't. Not Ned, not Robert. Certainly not Billy.

James stood up. He was done with being a coward. "Now what do I do?"

Miss Palmerton followed. "Now we must find the ring."

He drew in a breath. "Right. I assume it's on your hand?"

She said it was.

As he looked at her body, he couldn't see her hands, as they were tucked away under her. Nothing for it but to pull her out.

Shoving away the heebie-jeebies that crept across his shoulders, he took a hold of her waist and pulled. At first the decayed cloth of her gown came away in his hands. He shook it off as if they were spider webs. A second try shifted her body enough for him to reach an arm. By getting a firm grip on this, he was able to slide the body out from the crypt. Miss Palmerton's ghost cheered as her body was freed.

James laid the body out on the long grass. The struggle to free her had shredded her clothing into rags, leaving much of her body bare. She looked as if she'd only fallen asleep, only her chest did not move.

While he had been keeping company with a naked ghost for a couple of days, to see her body like that felt disrespectful. He shrugged off his green coat and laid it over her torso.

He lifted her cold, still hand. There, on her finger, was a little silver ring with a blue stone, like lapis. Surely something so small couldn't be enough to bring someone to the brink of death?

His fingers closed over the ring. He looked at her unmoving face. The ring was only supposed to cast her into a sleep. Yet it had separated her soul from her body. Was that death? Or was it only bodies that slept, and her soul, with nothing to do, wandered about?

He trembled in hesitation. If he removed the ring, would she be restored to life, like Miss Palmerton believed, or would it complete an act that was a hundred years overdue and kill her? Had she not been cursed and lived a normal life, she would have been dead before James had been born.

"James?" came her soft voice. "What's wrong?"

He looked up to her ghost. "What if this doesn't work? What if this kills you instead?"

She let her pale hand drift over his. "Would that be so bad?"

That took him aback. "You mean, after all your convincing me not to kill myself, you don't mind if you die?"

She moved closer to him so her form enveloped his. "You are full of life. Mine is a half-life. I am stuck between living and dead, and definitely stuck here at Stoweham. This is not the place for me. Please, James, remove the ring from my finger. Either I will live, or I will die. Either way, I will not have to face the horror of being left alone when..." her voice cracked, "When you leave."

"But I'm not leaving."

"Oh, yes you are," she insisted, fire igniting in her voice. "Stoweham is not the place for you, either. Regardless of what happens to me, you need to leave this place. Pack up your things and depart, never looking back. There is nothing but sorrow for you here."

His fingers had not moved from that ring. "But what if you die?"

"Then I die in the arms of the man I love."

A jolt of electricity ran through his body. What did she say? His hands froze on hers and on the ring. "You can't love me. We've only known each other for a few days."

"I've known you for years, James. Except when you were off to school, I've kept an eye on you."

Of course.

She continued, "Then one day you came home, and, unlike your forefathers, you never left again. Instead of heading out to the pub or whatever it is the young do today, you chose to remain home. You'd sit in the kitchen near the fire and read books by lamplight. I must thank you for reading in the rocking chair near the stove, for that meant I could hide in the walls and read the book over your shoulder. Though I would have preferred if you read something other than those adventure stories. A romance would have been nice."

James felt as naked as she appeared. "Were you always watching me?"

"Of course."

"Why didn't you say something? Why hide?"

"It would have been most inappropriate to show myself to a young boy. By the time you were of age, I…" Her face darkened into gray.

Was that how ghosts blushed?

"You were different. I can't tell you how much I wanted to say something." She shook her ghostly head. "Whenever I got the urge to speak with you, I'd run away. I thought if you knew about my presence, you'd flee, and then I'd never see you again." Her hand traced over his fingers. "And I so wanted to see you again. I didn't want to chance you rejecting me."

He released the ring, leaving it in place. "Tell me. Do you fall in love with all Cowper men, or just me?"

She tilted her head to the side. "I confess a fondness for you all. But since Lord Auberon, every generation has left here and returned with a bride. While I disapproved strongly of Miss Capel and her scheming ways, I cannot fault her sons, especially when I never had a chance to speak with them. Only you have I watched and never had to give up to someone else. I certainly wasn't going to let the Grim Reaper have you now."

"But you're ready to go to him yourself?"

She sighed. "In my century I have seen plenty of bodies buried in this graveyard, but none of them have come with ghosts. It's been very lonely here in the ether. I suspect the good have gone on to Heaven and the bad have descended to Hell. I am stuck in between. Please," she begged. "You want to be a man of courage. Pull off my ring."

A man of courage. What did that mean? That he jumped at every loud noise as if it was a gun in his ear? That he went to the recruitment office, knowing he would never pass, but going because it was expected of him?

Or did it mean going down to the Volunteer Corps training exercises in hopes that if only he maintained his stiff upper lip and fired a rifle he could prove once and for all that he wasn't a coward?

Prove to whom? Billy Forsythe? The village? Himself?

Whose job was it to declare a man a coward or not?

He looked up from her body to Miss Palmerton's ghost. Not once had she called him a coward. Not once had she scorned him. Granted, forcing his hand by telling Mother his secret plans was a bit underhanded. Yet he had come back. He'd opened a crypt and pulled out a body on the advice of a ghost. Not many men would have the courage to do that. "I'll do it," he said.

James took her hand, grasped the ring and before common sense could regain control of his actions, he pulled off the ring.

The ghostly image of Miss Palmerton disappeared before his eyes.

Chapter 4
Life Anew

Just like that, the ghost disappeared. No warning, no fading away, no last words. One moment she was there, then gone in the twinkling of an eye.

James looked down to Miss Palmerton's body. He squeezed the cold hand.

Nothing.

Ice settled in his veins as if his own heart had stopped. He'd killed her, just as he feared he would. Grief washed over him. He regretted telling her they'd only known each other for a couple of days. In the back of his mind, he'd always known she was there. Hadn't he dreamed of her often enough? Or at least, catching glimpses of her as he rose out of that dark mystery of sleep?

Had he been like the other young men in the village, who whispered tales of the bare-breasted, naked-limbed Stoweham Ghost, of how they yearned to spot her on her haunts?

And all this time she'd been right here, in his house, in his room. What would he have said, had she spoken to him earlier? Would he have taken the time to speak with her, or would he have run away? Or would he have treated her like an object, a spectacle to boast about to others?

There would be no more Stoweham Ghost.

The body drew a deep, sharp breath, quick and loud.

James dropped the hand and scuttled back through the grass.

Miss Palmerton exhaled with a soft sound, and then drew breath again. She sat up, startled. The coat slid to her lap. Her hand flew to her throat as she looked around. She saw James. The brightest of smiles lit her face. "It worked?"

He could only nod.

She felt her face with her hands, then the rest of her body. "Hah!" she cried out in joy. "It worked!"

Without any warning she launched herself at James, bowling him backward with a giant hug. Solid, real.

Hesitantly, he wrapped his arms about the now-warm, living body of Miss Palmerton. His coat had fallen off her and lay on the grass. The remains of her clothing hung in tatters from her limbs. Otherwise, it was the same, naked Miss Palmerton he'd always known.

She did not release him. Instead, she pressed her cheek to his and held it there. "I haven't touched anything in so long." Her hand stroked the other side of his face, feeling the sandpapery roughness of his five o'clock shadow. Then her fingers roamed upward to rustle through his wavy hair, disrupting it from its neatness. She sat up without warning. "How is my hair?" She poked at it and found a twig, which she removed in annoyance.

He studied her. When she was a ghost, he couldn't tell what shade her curly hair was, nor the color of her eyes. Her eyes were hazel. As for her hair, it was a dark blonde, except for one side, which was stained brown from the crypt. As she moved, bits of dirt fell away. Also, a smudge of dirt coated the same side of her face. This must have been how she reposed for a century.

James brushed at it with his thumb. "You could use a wash."

Miss Palmerton plucked at the remains of her afternoon gown. The dark fabric separated easily under her touch. "Alas. I am in need of clothing." In a moment of nostalgia, she gathered the tatters of fabric to her face. "I've missed fine gowns."

Ah, yes. Now that Miss Palmerton had rejoined the living, she would need what the living required. And James did not want to risk being caught out in a graveyard with a mostly naked young lady in his lap. Who knew what the villagers would say then? "Shall we get you back to the house?"

****

With James' green sack coat about her, and her tattered walking shoes still intact enough to protect her feet, Miss Patterson made it back to Stoweham House without incident. Sneaking her in was also not a problem, for her newly-restored body had no problems slipping in the front entrance and up the main staircase.

First, he took her to the bathroom. "I recommend you bathe."

He plugged the tub and turned on the taps, adjusting them to a warm temperature. He found Mother's lavender soap and placed it in the soap dish. He never used it, for he found the scent too feminine. Perhaps Miss Palmerton would enjoy it?

Meanwhile, she roamed the bathroom, touching every surface, from the tiles on the wall to the terrycloth towels. His coat only just covered her in the barest minimum of modesty. "I'd forgotten how things feel." She inhaled. "And how they smell." Her fingers went to her lips. "And food. I can eat food again!"

A dressing gown. She'd need a dressing gown for after the bath. The only one available was his. It would have to do. He fetched it while she explored the flavor and texture of the tooth powder. By the time he returned, the tub had filled sufficiently and he turned off the tap. "Take your time," he said. "I'm sure you've missed a good, hot soak."

The tub intrigued her. "Can't say that I have, for our tub was a little copper thing." She dabbed her fingers in the water. "Though I could get used to a bath every day, if you have such warm water at your beck and call."

He confessed to himself that he'd not given much thought to the boiler system that enabled hot water for the kitchen below and this bathroom above. He was too young to remember when plumbing had been installed in Stoweham House, though Mother praised the luxury of a hot bath frequently. And here was Miss Palmerton, equally grateful. No doubt she was as equally grateful when he'd showed her the water closet earlier, though he definitely did not stick around to hear her opinion. "I am going to look for something suitable for you to wear."

His sister Joan's old clothing might still be up in the attic. When she married just before the War, she insisted on a completely new trousseau, leaving her debutante wardrobe behind.

His face flushed. "I'll wait for you in my—in the bedroom." That was another thing. Where would she stay? What would she do? Her life had been interrupted for a hundred years. One couldn't simply pick up and carry on from where one left off. James saw some serious discussion ahead.

These thoughts tumbled through his head as he raided trunks in the attic. Joan had never thrown anything away and Mother insisted the maids dust up here every week. It wasn't that Mother was sentimentally attached to things the way Joan was, but that Mother detested an untidy house, even in the attic. Yes, he found Joan's clothing, including some more, ah, personal items. These he collected as well, deliberately not giving them much thought. He blessed his sister and her hoarding ways.

Thus accoutered, he descended from the attic. As he came down to the second floor, he heard the sounds of muffled singing. He did not fight the smile that played his lips. Of course she was happy.

His pleasure evaporated as he turned the corner into the corridor. There, ear pressed to the bathroom door, stood Mother. He'd forgotten about her. She wore her lavender going-out dress, high-waisted and flowy. One hand clutched her gloves while the other lay on the door. Her back was to James.

"What are you doing?" he asked her.

She jumped, dropping her gloves. "Oh, you startled me!"

He folded his arms about the clothing he brought. "I thought you were going out."

She ignored that. "There's someone in there."

He nodded. "The Stoweham Ghost is having a bath."

Her hands trembled, and she clutched them to her

chest. "Y-you mean th-the ghost from this morning?" Her voice wavered and tears filled her eyes.

Unbeknownst to the drama happening in the corridor, Miss Palmerton continued singing to herself.

James dropped the clothing to the floor and came up to Mother. He took her shaking hands in his. "Yes."

Her gaze darted to the door. "Why is she haunting the bathroom?"

He drew a breath. "Do you recall our conversation this morning?" Their painful, awkward, long overdue conversation. "Remember how you made me promise…" He couldn't say it. Mother had cried hard at the thought that she could have lost her only son. She made him promise to live, if only to spare her poor, widowed heart.

She nodded. The tears spilled out her eyes. She pressed her lips together but it didn't do her any good. A sob wracked her body.

His heart went out to her. He had never meant to hurt her. Other than Miss Palmerton, she was the only person in the whole village that did not hold him in some form of contempt. He drew her in an embrace. Oh, his poor mother. His ostracism in the village had been a heavy burden, but his death would have been worse still.

As he held her shuddering form, he murmured into her hair, "The ghost refuses to leave my side because she wants me to live. As long as she's here, I…" A thought trickled into his head. He was not ready to tell Mother the whole of Miss Palmerton's tale. But if Mother took comfort in her presence, maybe he would have found a place for Miss Palmerton to stay, at least until they sorted out a few things. "Everything will be all right." He gave a filial kiss to the top of Mother's head.

She nodded. "If you say so." She sniffed and pulled away, digging in her sleeve for a handkerchief. "I know about the Stoweham Ghost. It may be all well and good that she is watching over you, but couldn't you at least persuade her to find some clothing?"

For the first time that day, indeed, in a long time, James laughed.

****

Mother was on her way out. Aunt Violet, who had been waiting downstairs all this time, had persuaded Mother that going out for low tea would be just the thing to lift her spirits after this morning. Reassured that her son was safe under the watchful eye of the Stoweham Ghost, she departed, much to James' relief. At least he'd have an hour or two in which to sort out Miss Palmerton.

In his bedroom he laid out the clothing neatly on the bed. Back and forth he paced the room while he gathered his thoughts. Aunt Violet had taken over Joan's bedroom. Mother still occupied the master suite, while he remained in his childhood bedroom. Technically, as the Cowper heir, he should be in the master suite, but the thought had made him uncomfortable. Perhaps that was a good thing. The master suite, at the far end of the corridor, may have been too far for Miss Palmerton's ghost to go comfortably, not that that was an issue any longer.

This was the country seat of a gentle family, with plenty of rooms for guests. While they had been left unused for quite some time, a bit of freshening would see one fit enough for Miss Palmerton.

His bedroom door opened quickly, startling him. A robed Miss Palmerton darted in and closed it. She paused, listening for pursuit.

"My aunt and mother have gone out," James said. "Nobody will disturb us."

His voice startled her, but she soon relaxed. "I confess some awkwardness. I've forgotten how things worked." She told how she'd walked into the bathroom door in an absent-minded moment. "I was distracted by the softness of your dressing gown." She ran a hand over its collar before lifting it and sniffing it. "Is this what you smell like?"

James' heart beat harder. Now that she was clothed, even informally, his blood stirred. The thought of his dressing gown against her bare skin suggested things he'd not thought about for quite some time. After she'd had her fill of his scent from his robe, she approached him. Drawing near, she stood on tiptoes and pressed her nose to his neck. She inhaled deeply. The movement of air over his skin sent thrills through him.

Her arm slid about his waist. "Yes, this is how you smell." Her hand ran over his face. "And this is how you feel." That hand moved to the back of his head. "But how do you taste?"

He trembled as she pulled his head down to hers. Her lips touched his, soft and gentle. He had only a moment to draw a breath when she took his mouth with hers.

That was no maidenly kiss. Her lips parted, teasing at his, enticing him to open to her.

He closed his eyes and gave in. The thought that someone desired him intoxicated his senses. He'd forgotten what it was like to be wanted. Old desires he had shoved away knocked off the dust of their abandonment and sprang forth hot and true. Yes, he wanted her. He so wanted her. All his adolescent daydreams of the Stoweham Ghost rushed up. She was here, she was real, and she was kissing him.

She pushed him back until his legs hit the bed. Only then did she break contact. With a wicked gleam in her eyes, she bounced up onto the bed, heedless of the neatened clothing there. She drew him forward. "It's been so long since I've touched another human being. I want to explore everything. I want to explore you."

His head spun. She reached out to the buttons on his shirt.

She'd had them half-undone when a sobering thought intruded itself in the heat of the moment. "Wait," he said, his hands removing hers from his clothing. "I…I don't know if I can do this." The words tumbled out, a confession he had never thought he'd make. "I don't have experience. I mean…" Why did this have to be awkward? "I know I'm supposed to know what I'm doing, but I don't."

She gave him a fond smile. "Don't worry. I do."

That surprised him. "How? I thought debutantes were supposed to be pure and innocent."

"Indeed they are. However, haunt a place long enough and one will see things. You'd be surprised how many couples slip out to the cemetery for a bit of privacy, thinking that nobody would ever go there. I may not have practical experience, but I can't consider myself ignorant in such matters." She knelt on the bed and leaned over to him. "I've always wanted to try those things I've seen."

He gasped as she placed his hands on her soft, round breasts.

"Miss Palmerton," he stuttered as he attempted to remove his hands.

She refused to let him go.

"Shh," she replied. "To you, I am Georgia."

"I—"

"Say it. Say my name."

He swallowed and tried it on for size. "Georgia?"

"Yes, James. Try it again."

"Georgia." He rolled it around. "Georgia. I don't know." He tried to extract his hands once more. How many times had the village boys talked about being able to touch the breasts of the Stoweham Ghost? Yet here he was. It didn't seem right.

No, that wasn't it. Touching her felt more than right. He let his hand slide past her breast, around her rib cage to settle on her back. He wanted to draw her close. She let him as she deepened her kisses. When her tongue touched his, he jerked back in surprise, but she wouldn't let him escape. Her mouth molded to his, and he liked it. He liked it very much.

It was the thought of all the other boys, so many generations of boys, who had lusted after her that bothered him. She was his. She'd always been his. Even when he wasn't aware she was watching him. She had chosen him, even over the previous generations of Cowper men. With the exception of his too-many-great grandfather Lord Auberon, whenever a Cowper man had sought a bride, she'd stepped aside and never said a word. Yet when he sought to court death, she definitely interfered.

Miss Georgia Palmerton very much wanted James

Cowper. Who was he to resist?

How had she ended up in his lap? For that's where she was. Her hands ran over his bare chest, surprising him. When had she undone his shirt? The tie of the dressing gown had come loose. She shrugged it off her creamy shoulders. They looked very different now, all flush with life. He pressed his lips to them, smelling the scent of lavender. Perhaps he should find her some rose-scented soap, or maybe violets. Yes, violets would be nice.

Her hand slipped lower between them to tug at the waistline of his trousers.

That brought his focus back. He lifted his head. "We shouldn't be doing this."

"Absolutely we should." She rose up on her knees. With the weight of her newly-restored body, she bore him down to the bed. "You can't give me one solid reason why we shouldn't."

"We're not married." Yes, it sounded old-fashioned, but it was the only reason of which he could think.

"Not a problem," she replied. "We can fix that tomorrow. I know the parish priest."

With deft fingers that moved with surprising skill, she'd all but disassembled the remains of his clothing. His nether region strained to be free of the strictures clothing and circumstance had imposed. A knock on the door rang out before she could free him completely.

"James?"

They both froze, their heads turning to the door. "I thought you said your mother went out," she whispered to him.

He spread his arms in bafflement. "She had," he

whispered back.

"Are you in there?" Mother called out. Then the doorknob rattled.

The shock of potential discovery ran through him. He sat up. He would have risen completely to fumble at his clothing, but Miss Palmerton—Georgia—kept him pinned.

She called out, "I will have you know James is doing fine."

Silence from the other side of the door. The doorknob rattled once more, but the door did not open. Had he locked the door? He must have. He didn't recall doing it, and Georgia might not have realized it could be done. After all, she had walked straight into the bathroom door earlier, having forgotten she couldn't walk through walls anymore.

Then the tremulous voice of his mother called out, "Is that you, ghost? Are you in there?"

Another voice, too low for him to make out, murmured from the other side of the door. Sounded like his aunt.

"I am," Georgia replied. "And I tell you, James is fine." She ran a hand over his chest. "So very fine," she murmured low, just for him.

He stopped her hand. "I'm all right, Mother. You're back early."

A knock rang out on the door. "She's worried about you," came the no-nonsense tone of his aunt.

Carefully, James extracted himself from Georgia. Before he could free himself completely, she quietly hopped off the bed and padded over to the door.

Up close and personal to the barrier between his embarrassment and his mother, she said, quite strongly,

"Go away or I shall haunt your nightmares."

Mother and Aunt Violet must have been listening with their ears to the door. Georgia's strong voice so close to the door had to have startled them, for there was a scuffling and the sound of quick retreat.

A satisfied Georgia returned to bed. "Where were we?"

James didn't know what to say. "Did you just frighten away my mother?"

She climbed on and straddled him once more. "Did you really want her eavesdropping?"

He blushed. "No, but——"

"Is this not your house in name and deed?"

He had never given it much thought after the inheritance from his father but, "Yes."

"Then you can do whatever you want in your house." With desire shining in her eyes, she slowly drew down his waistband, peeling it back from his hips. "I intend to show you exactly what you can do in your own house."

Miss Palm—Georgia, proceeded to do just that.

Chapter 5
Making Plans

The next morning James woke with the impression of being watched. He found Georgia's naked form snuggled up next to his naked form, her hazel eyes observing him.

"Good morning," she said, rising up on an elbow before yawning. "I had forgotten how much I missed sleep."

James had forgotten how much he'd missed human contact. Georgia's contact throughout the night had kept him up in so many ways until they both collapsed from exhaustion. He needed that. Before she could run her fingers over his chest, his stomach growled.

"Ooh," she exclaimed, before resting her ear against his belly. "I'd forgotten about breakfast!"

His stomach hadn't. It complained loudly, for he had completely missed supper last night. He had vague recollections of someone knocking on his door, something about a tray, and him growling, "Go away!"

The thought of food gave Georgia fresh energy. She slid to the edge of the bed and fell off, exclaiming in surprise when she landed on the floor.

James scrambled over. "Are you all right?"

She assured him she was. "I'd forgotten about legs and how they tangled in bedclothes." Then she said, "Goodness. Are these for me?"

Her fall forgotten, Georgia had found the clothing James had brought down last night, and which had been subsequently knocked off the bed during their passion.

They had slipped his mind. "We can't have you roaming Stoweham naked, now, can we?"

She shrugged. "Hasn't been a problem for the past hundred years…" Her voice trailed off. She stroked the texture of the cotton fabric of his sister's blouse. "Clothes were one thing I missed very, very much."

James helped her to standing. He drew her close. "I promise to keep you well and truly clothed." He placed a kiss on the tip of her nose.

"Except when it is to our benefit to be unclothed." A smile played her lips. As she rose up on tiptoe to kiss him, his stomach growled and hers answered. She laughed.

He couldn't help but respond in kind. "You said something about breakfast?"

While they stared in bafflement at the women's clothing strange to them both, James wondered about his next step. One day he was ready to end his existence; the next day Georgia came into his life. He liked how her name rolled off his tongue, and how her tongue played with his. She must have witnessed quite a few illicit interludes over the years, for while her movements were clumsy and unpractised, she did know what she was about. Not that he'd know any different.

One thing was sure: his life in Stoweham could not remain the same. He'd given much thought that morning to things she'd said. He would have to make some hard decisions.

Eventually Georgia was clothed. His sister had been longer-limbed than Georgia, and more boyish. The long brown walking skirt strained over her hips in a suggestive manner. Thankfully, the cream blouse in all its ruffles hid that sin, even its snugness across her bosom was delicately hidden. As they wandered downstairs, the delicious scent of bacon drifted upward. She inhaled deeply. "I recognize that smell."

In her eagerness, she dashed down the stairs, holding up her skirt to keep from tripping. Her feet were bare, for Joan's shoes were a little large, and Georgia's original slippers were tatters. She made no sound in her descent.

James hastened after her. The last thing Mother and Aunt Violet needed was another morning scare from the Stoweham Ghost. He caught up with her just outside the breakfast room. "We go in together, and calmly."

Georgia agreed and took his arm. Thus, they promenaded in to the pale, lacy breakfast room. Still, her presence startled the occupants, seated around the round table.

Mother recovered first. "Goodness." A hand fluttered to her chest. "Imagine a ghost twice for breakfast." She lifted her spoon and took a bite of scrambled egg as if this was an everyday occurrence. Only the slight trembling of her hand betrayed her nerves.

Aunt Violet stared at her sister-in-law, her mouth agape.

Mother ignored her.

James felt Georgia's excitement over a prospect as simple as breakfast. He had to admit, the scent of bacon and buttered toast did smell good. "Mother, Aunt Violet, may I present Miss Georgia Palmerton, formerly the Stoweham Ghost, who has haunted our house and the church for the past hundred years."

Mother extended her hand out of habit, but hesitated. In nervousness, her fingers closed. "Pleased to meet you."

Georgia flashed her a genuine smile and tendered a curtsey. "Charmed." She studied his mother. "I have watched you for years, Helen, ever since Earnest brought you here."

"Oh." Mother sighed and clutched her hands at the mention of her late husband.

Aunt Violet's mouth remained open.

Mother offered, "I am glad you have found something suitable to wear. I declare you look almost human."

Georgia offered her a genteel curtsey. "Thank you." She plucked at the skirt. "I may have to find something more modern."

Only now did Aunt Violet speak. "If you can wear clothes, why did you haunt the village in the, the—" She blushed and swallowed.

Georgia didn't answer. Her gaze flickered to James.

He ruminated on this one. What to say to Mother? As he looked at Georgia Palmerton, his head spun with the possibility of his future. Something about last night tickled the back of his head. Oh yes. He had mentioned they weren't married, and she said they could fix that.

Was...was that a proposal of marriage? The more he thought about it, he figured, why not? Assuming she would have him. Aw, what was he thinking? Of course she would have him. What a lovely thought. He relaxed. "When Georgia was a ghost—"

"Georgia?" Aunt Violet exclaimed.

He ignored her outburst. "When she was a ghost, she had no choice over how she looked." He inhaled. He glanced over to Georgia for implicit permission to share her story.

She gave him an encouraging smile.

"But now that she lives once more, she can..." How to put it? Wear clothes? Eat food? Keep him up all night with wave after wave of sensual passion?

Aunt Violet shook her head. "What do you mean, 'lives'?"

Mother had pressed a fist to her lips as she listened to this interplay. How much did she know about the Stoweham Ghost? She didn't grow up here, unlike Aunt Violet.

Georgia, nonplussed by Aunt Violet's reaction, eyed the dish of coddled eggs on the table. "Give me a plate of those, and I'll tell you the whole story."

At first nobody moved. Then Mother grabbed the plate that was meant for James and ladled eggs onto it. She shoved it in front of Georgia. "Start from the beginning. Don't leave anything out."

First things first, of course. The moment that plate of eggs ended up in front of Georgia, her eyes lit up and she dug into them so fast her fork was almost an inconvenience.

"Mmm," she hummed over a mouthful of eggs. She chewed and closed her eyes, leaning back to enjoy the first meal she'd had in a century.

James watched her in her delight. He'd seen that expression before. He looked at her eggs. Surely they were the same ordinary eggs Cook's hens laid every day. Discarding propriety, he stabbed a bit of egg with a fork and lifted it to his own lips.

Imagine if he hadn't eaten eggs—or anything really—in such a long time. For the first time, he gave real consideration to the flavor of eggs. It was…eggy. Rich, buttery with just enough salt to bring out the flavor. He made a note to tell Cook how wonderful her eggs were. Had he ever truly thanked her for anything? Perhaps it was time to start.

Only after Georgia had polished off half her plate did she begin her story. Like Mother asked, she didn't leave anything out, even telling her things she'd not told him yet. He learned when and where she was born, who her parents were and when she came out. She spoke of how she esteemed Lord Auberon and how her family considered him a capital fellow.

But not once did she ever speak of love. James mulled this over. That she liked Lord Auberon, that was certain. But had she loved him? A quiet corner of James' heart hoped she hadn't. She didn't mention the kiss.

Then she told of one-sided rivalry and the subsequent deception which led to her century-long sleep. Her body slumbered while her soul roamed Stoweham.

By now even Aunt Violet had tears in her eyes. "How very sad. I wonder what happened to your rival?"

Only then did James realize Georgia had left out Charlotte Capel's name. Aunt Violet had a bit of family pride, even if the title and the townhouse ended up with cousin Reggie. Perhaps Georgia knew this and sought to spare Aunt Violet the dreadful news of her something-great grandmother's betrayal.

"So I had a bit of time to roam about." Georgia also shared her limited movements while a ghost. "Not much else to do, really, when one has half a house, a graveyard and a parish church." Her eyes settled on the cozy. "Is that tea?" Not that she waited for confirmation. She tipped the pot over her cup until it filled with steamy, comforting tea. She stirred in a spoonful of sugar, lifted the cup to her lips, sipped, and sat back with a happy sigh.

Mother drew a shuddery breath. "So your body has been hidden in the graveyard this whole time? How did...that is, how were you rescued?"

Georgia, still sipping her tea, looked to James. Let him finish the story.

He gazed at Mother. She'd had several shocks over the past twenty-four hours, and she'd soldiered on. Then and there, he promised he'd never do anything to break her heart again. At least she deserved the truth. "I had gone to the graveyard with the intention of killing myself."

Aunt Violet drew a breath. He'd forgotten she didn't know about his attempt. Aunt Violet looked over to Mother, who avoided her sister-in-law's gaze.

He continued on. "But Georgia saved my life. In return, I saved hers. I found her body, pulled her out, and removed the cursed ring."

The ring! Where did he put it? It was too dangerous to leave lying about. He patted his pockets. Nothing. "Georgia?" he fought rising anxiety. "Do you remember where I put the ring?"

Her teacup frozen half-way to her lips, she shook her head. "I...lost consciousness for a moment when you removed it."

He dashed from the table. What if it was in yesterday's clothes? Had the maid-of-all-work been in to tidy his room yet?

To his relief, no, she hadn't tidied the room, and he had found the ring tucked into his waistcoat pocket, next to his watch. The waistcoat had been tossed to the floor when Georgia had taken him apart last night. He placed the ring on his bureau. He would have to figure out what to do with it later.

How did one uncurse a ring?

With relief, he returned to the breakfast room. There, Georgia had loaded up her plate once more. But no one conversed. Between Georgia, Aunt Violet, and Mother, nobody said a thing. Georgia ate in silence. Aunt Violet looked away, and Mother had her hands folded tightly in her lap.

"What happened?" he asked.

Aunt Violet shaded her eyes with her hands. Mother looked away. Georgia's fork slowed. "Your mother asked a question that I did not know how to answer."

"Oh, what now?"

Georgia reached for her teacup. "She asked, 'What now?' It wasn't my place to tell her. Nothing's been made official yet."

That got Mother's attention. "What's not been made official?"

Georgia looked up at him apologetically. "See? How do I answer that?"

Mother's hands came down firm on the table. "What's not official yet?"

James felt heat rush to his face. He swallowed, his throat suddenly dry. He took Georgia's teacup from her hands and gulped it down, in spite of its heat.

"I've told James, for his safety and sanity, he needs

to leave Stoweham. Possibly for good," said Georgia.

James choked on the tea. He had expected her to declare their intention to marry. But yes, leaving Stoweham was also on the cards.

"Leave Stoweham?" echoed Aunt Violet.

"He can't stay. You know he can't."

"But...why?"

James coughed as he sat down. He'd emptied the teacup. Alas, the teapot was now drained. "I'm not welcome here."

Mother sniffed. "But you live here. You were born here."

"It's your heritage," said Aunt Violet.

"Mother, you weren't born here. Why should I stay?"

It was Aunt Violet who answered. "Because you're a Cowper."

"Cousin Reggie lives in town. I don't see you berating His Lordship on where he lives."

"You can't just leave!" Aunt Violet's voice rose in pitch.

He pushed away his teacup. "That's what I once thought. I didn't know I could leave, and I knew I couldn't stay. Is it any wonder I thought death was my only escape?"

A sob escaped Mother.

"Sorry, Mum." But it was true. He'd been so connected to the thought of Cowpers in Stoweham, he thought the only way to leave for good was feet first. And then to spend the rest of eternity moldering away in a grave less than a mile from where he was born.

Had he never realized that if he'd succeeded in enlisting, he would have been sent to Europe like all the other young men of Stoweham? Or did he blithely think he'd come home by Christmas? Not everyone who left had returned to Stoweham. Those who did had left something of themselves behind. Two days ago many of them blamed him for their lost humanity.

He bowed his head. "If it were just me, I'd be up and gone in a trice. But it doesn't work like that." He looked at Mother. She still clenched her hands in her lap. "For months we've been fretting over the finances. This drafty old house has been eating away at our capital. We can't do that much longer." Plus the war didn't help. "I propose we sell Stoweham House and move to London."

"WHAT?" Mother and Aunt Violet exclaimed at the same time.

Aunt Violet fanned herself with her hand. "We can't sell it!"

"We can do whatever we want," James countered. "It's not entailed."

Tears streamed down her face. "But it's been in the family for generations!"

"And it would leave the family after my generation if we stay here." The topic of him being the end of the Cowper line had never been openly discussed before, even when Mother mourned the unmarried state of her son. About time it was brought up.

"You don't have to be the last," Georgia said.

His glace stole sideways to Georgia. His line didn't have to end with him. He hadn't really discussed it with her, not that they had discussed much since before he'd brought her back to life.

She laid a warm hand on his. "I have no desire to remain in Stoweham. However, I would like it very much if I could remain with you."

His heart thumped at what she was suggesting. "You mean that?"

She nodded. "Everyone I knew is gone. The only living souls who have treated me proper are you." She looked about the breakfast room. "Indeed, the only living souls who have treated you proper are here."

This was true.

"We cannot stay," James said to Mother. "We can't afford to maintain Stoweham House and a place in town. If you wish to stay in Stoweham village, then you can. We'll find you a nice little cottage closer to town where you and Aunt Violet can keep each other company. But we must sell Stoweham House."

Mother had grown silent in that pursed-lip way of hers.

Aunt Violet's lips were also pursed, but in anger. "I won't let you do it," Aunt Violet stated in a tight voice.

Before James could reply, Georgia stood up. "Perhaps we should let them think about it," she suggested. "After all, you did propose to sell her childhood home." She tugged at his sleeve.

He looked from Aunt Violet, attempting to kill him with a glare, to Mother, who didn't meet his gaze. She had not lost that unhappy set to her mouth, but her eyes had moved on to thoughtfulness. She didn't grow up here. Perhaps she would see reason. Not that James needed either lady's permission to sell the house. Still, he would prefer to do it with their blessing, or at least without too many hard feelings. Georgia was right. They needed to let the family think about it.

Before he left the breakfast room, James snagged the dish with the remaining scrambled eggs. After all, breakfast was important if one was going to change one's life.

Once he had a bit of food in him, James felt better prepared to face the world, or at least face the rest of his life. For that was what he had to determine that morning. Having declared his intent to sell Stoweham House and leave the village for good, he needed to decide what his next step was.

Georgia insisted they go for a walk. "Will do us some good. Clear the cobwebs and give us some space."

Two pairs of socks made his sister's shoes fit Georgia sufficiently, so off they went.

She hooked her arm through his and guided James, none too subtly, in the direction of St. Mary's. "I wish to speak with the parish priest."

With Vicar Johnson? "What are you going to say to him?"

"First, I am going to give him a piece of my mind. All these years he's been here, he could have helped me. But instead he treated me like some sort of demon. Refused to listen to me every time I came to ask for help."

"Don't know why," James murmured, a small smile on his face.

Georgia dug in her heels. "Are you saying I'm frightening?"

"Absolutely."

Georgia opened her mouth, thought better of it, and resolutely marched on, her initial thought unvoiced. After a few moments musing, she said, "I don't know if it's a good thing or a bad thing that the vicarage is, was outside my comfortable range, or I would have haunted him to insanity."

"I suppose it would have been his own fault."

"Indeed."

James let a chuckle rise within him. "So after you've had it out with the vicar, then what?"

"Well," she said, her voice dropping soft. "That all depends on you."

"Oh?"

She looked up at him. "You've been dropping subtle hints about, shall we say, a long-term arrangement?"

Georgia couldn't have meant anything other than marriage. "So have you," he replied.

They stopped just before the gate to the grounds of St. Mary's, under the shade of an elm tree. He took both her hands in his. "While we have been watching each other our whole lives, well, my whole life, we've only really become acquainted these past few days."

She tilted her head sideways, an eyebrow cocked in puzzlement. A few larks twittered in the tree above them.

He ran his thumbs over her knuckles. "Please don't think me too forward in suggesting the possibility of marriage." He pushed the words out quickly before they had a chance to get stuck in his throat. "Some would say that it's rather early, but ours hasn't exactly been a straightforward connection, has it?"

"Certainly not traditional. Do you regret that?"

He shook his head. "I only worry what people would say."

She smoothed her features. "Which people?"

He hesitated. "Well, people in the village." He turned his gaze toward St. Mary's. Beyond that was the village.

She scoffed at that. "Since when is their opinion worth more than yours?" She let out a strangled noise. "Since when is their opinion worth anything at all? They surely have not treated you the way you deserve. For a village once beholden to the Cowpers, they've done a good job of forgetting their roots."

"They're still beholden to the Cowpers," he answered with a quieter voice.

That made her blink. "Are they? But you've been having financial troubles ever since your father died. If they're beholden and you're collecting the rents, where does the money go?"

"Cousin Reggie."

"What? That pompous fellow? Why, he hasn't been up to Stoweham House in the past five years."

James didn't miss him much. "He is Lord Cowper. With the exception of Stoweham House and its gardens, the rest of the property belongs to him."

"Yet he's been living it up in the London townhouse? Why couldn't you have had the townhouse, and he rusticated here instead?"

He pressed her warm hands close to his chest. "And miss out saving you?"

Only then did she look up into his eyes, abashed. "I'd forgotten about that."

He leaned forward and pressed a kiss to her nose. "Alive only two days and she's already forgotten the past century."

She made a face. "Trying my best to do just that." She turned toward St. Mary's. "You mentioned marriage?"

"So I did."

She looked back. "Are you asking me?"

"I am."

She considered it. She frowned and exhaled and tilted her head. "You know, it is the best and most direct marriage proposal I have ever received. I accept."

A smile of delight broke out on his face. She returned it before nearly bowling him over with an enthusiastic kiss.

When she finally let him come up for air, she said, "And now we must speak with Vicar Johnson. I shall hound him until he agrees to read our banns as soon as possible. After all, he owes me one Very Big Favor."

James agreed to let Georgia go first. After all, this was her grudge to settle with Vicar Johnson and a century of his predecessors.

St. Mary's Chapel was a beautiful building of warm local stone. The stained glass windows that had been lost during the Reformation had been lovingly restored by one of James' ancestors. Since then, it had served the parish of Stoweham.

He waited in the south aisle while Georgia stalked to the north chapel and the vestry to confront Vicar Johnson.

Vicar Johnson, a rotund man with the booming voice necessary to address an entire congregation, came waddling out of the lady chapel, the remaining wisps of his white hair streaming behind him. "Oh, no!" he called out, his plain vestments flapping against his legs. "Out you go, ghost. I'll not have your kind here. This is a house of the Lord." He waved his fingers at her as if she was an erring cat who could be shooed away.

Georgia Palmerton would not be shooed away. She stood right in the middle of the church, folded her arms and said, "No."

Vicar Johnson came to a halt, considered the rebellion before him, then hastened off again. James leaned out from the south aisle. Had she driven him away with a single word?

But no. Back he came, a silver jug of water in his hands. As he hurried up to her, he dipped his fingers in and flicked them at her. Georgia, to her credit, stood her ground. She rolled her eyes as the parish priest flicked water all over her. When she refused to budge, he came before her.

He considered the jug in his hands. He looked up at her. "Why are you wearing clothes?" he asked, baffled.

"Because every time I show up naked, you chase me away."

He squinted at her. "Wait. You're not a ghost."

"Not anymore," she replied. Then she took the jug from his hands.

While he gaped at her, she dashed the entire contents of holy water right in his face.

From the aisle James exclaimed before clamping a hand over his mouth. This was Georgia's fight.

A very wet priest sputtered in surprise.

"How dare you leave me there for a hundred years!" Her fists balled up and her face reddened in fury. "I've been laying out in that graveyard for a century waiting for someone to free me from some awful enchantment."

Vicar Johnson's face turned purple. His mouth worked up and down, but no words came out.

She plucked at the clothes on her form. "It was not my fault I appeared undressed. You know the saying, 'We come into this world with nothing, and we leave with nothing?'" She held out her arms. "Literally, we leave with nothing." She shook a finger in his face. "All you, or any of St. Mary's priests, had to do was come find me, and you could have freed me. Instead, you all were so wrapped up in your 'avoid the appearance of evil' that you never thought I might have been the victim of something awful? Honestly, did you really think the whole purpose of my appearance was for your titillation?"

A tiny little nag of guilt tugged at James' heart. What Stoweham man, young or old, had not considered that angle? Now that he thought about it, it had been rather unfair for Georgia. They'd all spent their time looking for her naked form and not giving a single thought to the person behind the form. He vowed he'd never think of her as an object again.

The vicar lifted a shaking hand, and swiped out at her. Expecting the incorporeal ghost, he jerked back his hand when it came into contact with Georgia's shoulder. He retreated several steps. "You're not a ghost."

She advanced on him. "Not any more. You know who rescued me? James Cowper."

Vicar Johnson huffed. "What? That coward?"

James stiffened. Even the priest scorned him? Regardless of what Mother said, being called a coward by the parish priest sealed away any doubts James had about leaving Stoweham.

Georgia laughed derisively. "Of all the men in a hundred years, only he had the courage to remove a ring from the hand of a corpse."

The vicar inhaled sharply through his nose. "Grave robbing?"

Georgia shook the jug in his face. "Rescue mission. Who else was brave enough to listen to the story of a ghost?"

Vicar Johnson had backed up so much his legs hit the edge of a pew. He sat down and didn't rise. "Ghosts don't come back from the dead."

She leaned in close. He didn't flinch away. "See, I wasn't really dead. Only enchanted." She rose up and spread her arms. "Whatever brave knight rescues the fair maiden may claim her hand in marriage."

Huh. James had never thought of it that way.

She raised a finger. "Now, seeing that I have been resident in Stoweham since, oh, before your grandfather was born, I think that clears the path for me quite nicely." She jabbed her finger at his wet cassock. "This is what you're going to do. You will call the banns for my wedding for three weeks. You will also ignore any protests anyone raises about my wedding—"

"I can't do that!"

She chuckled, a cold sound. "Oh, you will do whatever I tell you to do. See, I know your secrets." With that, she leaned over and whispered in his ear.

Vicar Johnson's countenance paled.

Of course she knew his secrets. Probably knew the secrets of everyone who'd come to confess as well. Now there was a powerful thought.

Maybe that's what was also going through Vicar Johnson's mind, for after she'd said her piece, he looked at her with horrified eyes. "What about the Seal of the Confessional?"

"That binds you, not me. Anyhow, I do not see why you have concerns. I have not asked you to do anything illegal or immoral. Quite the contrary. I insist you do your job. There is no impediment whatsoever to my marriage. Anyone who raises a protest will not have a leg to stand on."

The priest shook his head. "I won't do it. Nobody will believe you."

She chuckled. "Won't they?" She lost her humor. "Either you read the banns, or I go straight to the bishop and procure a common license." She drew close to him, but not so close James couldn't hear her. "If I have to go to the bishop, you better believe I will tell him everything."

He closed his eyes at this. "I'll need the groom's permission," he replied smugly.

"Not a problem," James replied, emerging from the south aisle. "I give it."

The vicar jumped at the sound of his voice. "I didn't see you there."

"No, you didn't." James came forward, his hand gliding over the backs of the pews. "How much support does St. Mary's receive from the Cowper family?"

Vicar Johnson stuttered for a moment. "The Cowpers have traditionally been very generous," he confessed.

Well, Lord Cowper had been very generous. Chances were cousin Reggie had no idea the family coffers regularly supported the church.

James came up and slipped an arm around the small yet solid waist of his wife-to-be. "Wouldn't it be a shame if that support came to an end, all because the local parish priest failed to recognize the Cowpers among his parishioners?"

Now Vicar Johnson paled so much James feared he might faint.

"I was baptised here," James prompted. "First communion, faithful follower, buried my father here. You cannot deny me to marry here when there is no impediment. Personal dislike does not count."

At this, the vicar dropped his head. "I'll read the banns." He refused to meet James' gaze.

"Good." James held out his arm to Georgia. "We look forward to hearing them next Sunday." Well and truly time to get out of the chapel.

As they were departing, Georgia had one last thing to say. "Consider this, Vicar, if I am married, I have no reason to haunt you any longer. Wouldn't it be nice to have your chapel back all to yourself?

The words Vicar Johnson muttered after them were not words a man of the cloth should say.

Chapter 6
Making War

James couldn't get away from St. Mary's soon enough. While the village's derision of him wasn't news, the vicar's opinion was a surprise. If it wasn't for the fact St. Mary's was his local parish, James would have been more than content to marry somewhere else.

"Slow down," Georgia begged.

Realizing he'd been moving at quite the pace, he dropped to a saunter. "Apologies."

"It's all right. It's only that I am feeling a bit...delicate this morning." She blushed as she said this.

"What?" said James, just before he caught her meaning. Then it was his turn to blush. "Oh. I didn't realize—"

She waved this away. "We both know it was my own fault. They say a woman's first time can leave her rather sore." And the second and the third and the fourth. For someone who'd never made love before, Georgia had been voracious. Even if she had been experienced, last night was enough to rub anyone raw.

"I'll be careful next time."

She smiled at this. "Oh, there will definitely be a next time." Then she stopped. "Wait. Where are we going?"

James looked up. His feet had not taken him back

to the house, but in the direction of the village. "Thought I'd get a newspaper. Perhaps I can find an advert for a selling agent."

Georgia hesitated. "Is it safe for you to go into town?"

He stopped. A house roof or two were visible from St. Mary's. "It's never safe. But one must go to fetch the paper. We must go to it."

"Couldn't you send a servant?"

James shook his head. "Can't spare one today, and shopping day was yesterday. I'm not waiting another week just so Cook can buy me a paper when she sets for town." He started again, but she didn't move. "What?"

"I just don't like you going into town." She raised gentle fingers to his cheek. "And you've still got a darkened daylight."

Yes. He'd been trying to avoid the thought of his black eye. "If I want a paper, I don't have much choice."

Then she smiled at him. "Of course you do. I could go into town and buy it for you."

Now it was his turn to be afraid. "You haven't been to town in a century."

"Pish-tosh. If you tell me where to go and what to do, I'm sure I could figure it out."

James sighed and gave in. He told her which papers to get at the greengrocer and how much it would cost then dug through his pocket for a few coins. "Hurry back. Someone might recognize you."

She lifted an eyebrow. "Dressed in clothes?"

"Fair point." Even if those clothes were alluringly tight across some of her best features.

He walked her nearly to High Street before letting her go. Then he hid behind a tree and waited.

Soon she sauntered back, two newspapers tucked under her arm. "I think I bemused Mrs. Rickets. When I was paying for the paper, I asked if her if little Dottie had recovered from the croup."

He blinked. "You spoke with her?"

"Of course. Didn't want to appear suspicious now, did I." She handed him a London newspaper and a Buckingham one. "So there she stood, answering my questions while wracking her brain to recall who I was. Ever so diverting."

Together they headed back to Stoweham House, discussing what needed doing if they were to leave the town for good. Sell the house, of course, regardless of whether Aunt Violet would agree. James was reasonably certain Mother would come around. Get married. The quickest and easiest way was out of St. Mary's. Only thing left was to purchase one-way train tickets, and they could knock the Stoweham dust off their shoes for good.

There wasn't much packing to be done, as the furniture would be sold along with the house. Just personal items, whatever mementoes Mother had kept—she was not one much for sentimental tokens—and clothes.

Georgia plucked at her blouse. "I hope I'm not mistaken for a servant in these older clothes when we get to London."

James promised her they'd visit a dressmaker once they got there.

Georgia hugged his arm. "Pick a knowledgeable one. I wouldn't know what was fashionable or not. She could dress me in a burlap sack, and I wouldn't know the difference."

When they reached the gate to Stoweham House, James paused. "There is one more thing. I need my Silver War Badge."

"What's that?"

He fingered his bare lapel. Georgia had offered to darn it up for him without asking the cause of the tear. "All men who present themselves for enlistment are eligible for a Silver War Badge. It's supposed to prevent you being handed your white feather."

"We'll be sure to pack it."

He shook his head. "I don't have it. It was…taken."

Georgia waved her hand dismissively. "We'll get you another one."

"No. They can't be replaced. Once you've been issued with yours, that's it. When it's gone, it's gone. If I don't have it, the same thing that happened here would happen elsewhere." He gathered her hands close to his chest. "I want a fresh start for both of us."

Ignoring the fact that Mother might be watching from the window, James kissed Georgia, and not a chaste peck as one would expect in public. However, he did stop her hands as they reached for the buttons of his waistcoat. "Now, now. Business first." He fetched the newspapers that had fallen from under his arm.

"Why?"

"Do you want to spend a minute longer in Stoweham than you have to?"

"No. But will an hour really matter?"

He arrested her hand which was sliding along his trouser front. "I recall the last time. We were up all night."

Georgia sported a mischievous grin. "So we were." As she pressed herself close, her hand eased into the back of his waistband.

James gave in. "At least wait until we get to the house and a proper bed."

"Why?" There would be no extinguishing that wicked gleam in her eye now.

"Because I do not wish to explain grass stains."

****

If their departure from Stoweham was to be delayed, James agreed that being in bed with Georgia was one of the best reasons. Like yesterday, she'd sent his senses reeling and made him glad she'd saved his life. It had been a pleasant afternoon, the first in a very long time.

As she rested her head on his shoulder, he played with her tangled curls. They still smelled of the lavender soap she'd used that morning. No matter how much she scrubbed, she couldn't remove the stain of the crypt from her hair. Thus, her locks were two-tone, one side brown where she had lain on it for a century, the other her natural blonde.

Another thing to think about: Georgia had absolutely nothing to call her own. He'd have to see to all those feminine tools: hair brushes, soap, face powder. What else? A toothbrush. What toiletries did Mother use? His sister's abandoned clothing would do until they got to London.

Georgia's fingers danced lightly over his chest. "A Silver War Badge," she mused. "Is that the little round pin you started wearing last year? About so big?" She held out her index finger and thumb.

"That's the one." It was a circular pin with the words 'For King and Empire—Services Rendered' surrounding a fancy Georgius Rex Imperator. No one could mistake a Silver War Badge for anything else.

"Hmm," she replied.

Her fingers drew circles on his skin. If she hadn't just worn him out, this light touch would have stirred him again.

"So if we could get our hands on one, perhaps a jeweller could copy it?"

He shook his head. "Each one is unique. They're numbered and the reason for discharge is listed on the back. It'd be a forgery if we were to copy one."

"I'm up for a little crime."

He stared at her.

"What?" she replied, her eyes all wide and innocent. "It's not like you're not entitled to wear one. All we need to do is make sure the jeweller puts the right number on the back. What is the number?"

Good question. He couldn't recall it off the top of his head, but it was listed on his certificate. "I recall the discharge code. It was KR: (ix). It meant 'Unfitted for the duties of the corps'."

"What? All because you fainted in the recruitment office?"

"Because the thought of handling a firearm terrifies me. If I can't handle a rifle, I'm all but useless as a soldier."

"What does KR nine mean?"

"King's Regulations number nine."

She settled back into the crook of his arm. "I'm still considering forgery. I say we borrow someone's badge, have it copied so it looks like your lost one, then quietly return it. No one will know but me, thee, and the jeweller who'd been paid to keep mum."

"And if he doesn't?"

"So what if he calls the Runners? They come to look at your badge, you show them the certificate, they confirm with the War Office that it is your badge. How will they tell it's a forgery?"

She had a point.

"So where are we going to get a war badge to copy?"

"Oh, I thought I'd borrow Billy Forsythe's badge. I believe he owes you a favor."

James' hand froze in her curls. "Billy doesn't have a war badge."

"Sure he does. I noticed it when I passed him in the village after I bought the newspaper. Saluted me with his stump." She wrinkled her nose. "It didn't impress me as much as he thought it would."

James sat up, causing Georgia to tumble into the sheets. "Oh, for the love of—Billy is the one who took my War Badge." He climbed out of bed and scrambled for his clothes.

"So if we were to take it from him, we wouldn't have to give it back. Also save us the trouble of dealing with a disreputable jeweller. Wait," she cried as he pulled on his trousers. "Where are you going?"

"To get my War Badge back."

She followed, snatching her clothes off the floor. "You can't go alone."

He'd done up the buttons of his shirt wrong and had to redo them. "There's no one to stand with me."

"I will."

He turned to her. She stood there, clothing in her

hands but otherwise as naked as she'd been for the past hundred years. "What can you do?"

"For starters, I can slap him for his impudence. Then I can spill his secrets and some to anyone who will listen."

James sank to the bed and located his shoes. "I think it'll take more than that."

She smiled at him. "That's what you're for." She located her underclothes. Despite having to think about how they worked, eventually she'd clothed herself. His sister's big, clunky shoes looked ridiculous on Georgia's delicate feet, but nothing could be done about that until London.

With a supportive Georgia by his side, James Cowper set off to get back his war badge.

****

Billy Forsythe's residence was a two-up two-down terrace house near the center of town. He'd married shortly before the war then left his young bride on her own while he served on the Continent. He was gone not quite two years before the injury sent him home. Some Stoweham men were still abroad. And a few would never make it home, with only a telegram to their families to impart the bad news.

James felt some guilt over that. Here he was, otherwise an ideal candidate, yet others would never see their loved ones again. He looked to Georgia who walked beside him with purposeful strides. She'd disappeared, never to see her family again. Her whole world was gone. Yet here she was, making the best of her new life. She had unwavering faith in him. He should have some in himself.

As it was getting on in the afternoon, James

expected everyone to head home for tea. It was not polite to call at tea time unless one was invited. James didn't care. Bolstered by Georgia's presence, he hammered on the door.

Billy's wife Ethel opened up. She was a short lass, with broad shoulders and narrow hips. She and Billy didn't have any children, nor did her belly look to be swelling with future little Forsythes. "Billy ain't here," she said. "He's at the pub."

A momentary wave of relief rolled through James. He hadn't realized how tense he'd been. "When's he back?"

Ethel Forsythe looked Georgia up and down. "Dunno. When he's ready, I suppose."

James spied something just inside the door, tucked into the umbrella stand. Without an invitation, he stepped inside and pulled it out. It was the dummy rifle from training the other day, good for little more than beating a man over the head. His head was still sore where the stock had grazed him. Lucky it hadn't knocked him out. James had a plan. He slung the rifle up onto his shoulder.

"Hey!" Ethel protested. "You can't have that."

Georgia stepped in front of Ethel. "He can do whatever he wants."

"Oy. Who are you?" Ethel tried to push past.

Georgia snagged Ethel's arm and whispered in her ear. Ethel stopped, listened, horror dawning on her face. "Where'd you hear that?"

"A little ghost told me."

Ethel wrapped one arm about her waist and clamped another hand over her mouth. Without further protest, she watched James and Georgia leave, refusing to go back into the house as long as they were within her sight.

Only after they turned the corner did James ask, "What did you say to her?"

"Never you mind."

James didn't press her. They had more important business.

As they walked along the darkening High Street, Georgia eyed the dummy rifle James carried across his shoulder. She opened her mouth, must have thought better of it, and closed it. She did this several times.

"It's not really a rifle," James explained. "It can't be fired. Essentially, it's little more than a club."

"So it's the noise of gunfire that frightens you?"

He nodded. Other loud, unexpected noises, like a door blowing shut in the wind, or thunder produced the same results.

They reached the pub. The Queen's Head was one of the few original Tudor buildings left in Stoweham, with its dark beams and whitewashed walls. The thatch had long been replaced with tiles.

James hesitated at the door.

Georgia looked at him sideways. "What are you thinking?" she asked.

James drew a deep breath. "I am about to take the most terrifying thing I know and use it against another man." He closed his eyes, fighting his conscience. "I can't do—shouldn't do—this sort of thing, but God help me, I must."

To his surprise, she slipped under his arm and put her arms about his waist in a comforting manner. "Sometimes you must do what needs to be done. Especially if it saves a life."

He words startled him. "Whose life?"

"Yours," she replied. "And mine, I suppose. Unless you retrieve your war pin, you will not be treated with respect in London."

He nodded. Time for some courage.

James pushed open the door of the pub and strode inside, Georgia right behind him. He had never liked the Queen's Head, with its low dark beams he had to duck and its too-close atmosphere. It was as if he was walking into a smelly, smoky box trap, a trap that would not only capture his body but his soul. How could anyone choose to spend night after night in a place like this? Yet that was what most of Stoweham's men did.

There, at the far end of the pub, sat Billy Forsythe, enjoying a pint with a few mates. They'd crowded around one of the ancient wooden tables, laughing at who-knew-what. Their voices filled the stuffy atmosphere, a cloying mockery to the coldness in his heart. Theirs was a jolly lot, until James arrived.

He did not hesitate, but strode in to the pub, straight up to Billy and levelled the rifle in his face.

Immediately the laughter ceased. Billy's mates stood up and backed away, the squeak of their chairs on the stone floor the only sound. Only Billy remained seated. Like rolling ripples on a pond, silence fell throughout the whole pub. The other patrons froze, cautious. To a man, they all knew James Cowper, knew him as a coward. What did they think, seeing him armed like this?

Billy froze, his gaze drawn to the barrel of the rifle.

James' voice was low and cool. "You have something of mine."

Billy didn't respond. James shoved the barrel right in his face.

That's when Billy fell back out of his chair. He scooted back, legs flailing in terror, pushing past the second table to cower in the corner.

As his rival scuttled away like a frightened spider, something shiny on Billy's lapel caught James' eye: his Silver War Badge. Billy had the stomach to wear it himself? Didn't his missing hand mark him enough? Or was it a spoil of war, to be flaunted in the face of the enemy?

Everyone in the pub rose to their feet as they watched loud, proud Billy turn into a trembling, sobbing wreck of a man.

James had heard of shell shock. But he never expected to see a case. Yet here was Billy crouched in a corner, crying like a baby with his arms thrown over his head.

Georgia moved first. She knelt down next to Billy. With gentle hands she removed the Silver War Badge from his lapel. Then she leaned in and whispered something. Billy's trembling stopped long enough for him to listen. He dropped his arms just enough to stare at her. The terror never left his eyes. Georgia rose and retreated, the Silver War Badge in her hand. Billy wrapped himself into a tight little ball.

James lowered the dummy rifle, no longer proud of the panic he'd unexpectedly ignited in this man. He even averted his gaze from the growing puddle on the floor beneath Billy.

Without a word, James and Georgia left the pub.

James left the dummy rifle just outside the Forsythes' door. It was no longer his problem.

Wordlessly, Georgia offered him his Silver War Badge. He repinned it to its usual place on his lapel. She slipped her arm around his. Together they returned to Stoweham House in silence.

Twilight had arrived by the time they got back, the driveway almost too dark to see. One by one the stars appeared in the firmament. James' heart was too cold to make a wish. Only the sounds of their feet crunching on the gravel and the evening breeze in the trees filled the air.

They didn't bother to go to the front door. Doubtless it had been locked for the night. Instead they went around to the kitchen door in back. James slowed as he descended the steps but Georgia kept going, straight into the door with a thud! James barely caught her rebounding form in time.

"Sorry." She gave him a guilty puppy-dog gaze. "I keep forgetting I'm solid now."

"I keep forgetting I'm human." His guilt twinged at his insides.

To their surprise, the kitchen door was yanked open by Cook, who let out a small shriek and slammed the door on them. James jumped back, startled, but the spots didn't appear before his eyes.

Georgia sighed. "I'm ready to forget this place and find a new life elsewhere."

James couldn't agree more.

They let themselves into the kitchen, Cook having fled, probably to give her notice. Georgia slipped her arm through James', a move he found comforting. Together they set off for the bedroom.

As they passed the parlor, Mother's voice called out, "James? Is that you?"

He sighed. "Yes, Mum."

"Could you come in here, please?"

He knew that voice. It was her "you're in trouble, young sir" voice. He hadn't heard that one since childhood. Releasing Georgia's arm, he went into the parlor. She chose to remain behind. Lucky her.

The parlor retained a shred of the dignity that was once Stoweham House. If any room reminded them of the place it once was, it was here. Elegant furniture with their beautifully carved dark wooden legs sat about the perimeter of the room. Thick, heavy curtains framed the tall windows, not yet drawn closed against the night. A small chandelier hung suspended from the ceiling. Although it had been wired for the electric lights, it remained off. Tall floor lamps illuminated the room instead, giving it a warm, comfortable glow.

There he found Mother seated on the sofa, with Aunt Violet on a chair opposite. Inwardly, he groaned. The last thing he wanted was another lecture.

At least she got straight to the point: "We're not letting you sell Stoweham House."

He folded his arms. "And I can't let you keep it."

Aunt Violet did not say a word, but her left eye twitched. Her hands lay clutched tightly in her lap.

Mother's hand rested on a foolscap folio that sat beside her. "While you were gone, I had a look at the finances." She drew out a piece of paper. "I know we're going backward financially. Stoweham House is too large for us; I realize that." She drew a breath as if summoning more courage. "I read through the newspaper you brought back. I don't know if you had seen the article on the Royal Bucks?"

He blushed. Georgia had thoroughly distracted

him; he never got around to reading that paper. "You mean the hospital in Aylesbury?"

She nodded. "It seems it's full. The article mentioned the Red Cross was looking for more suitable homes in the area to convert to auxiliary hospitals." She looked about the spacious parlor. Granted, the furnishings hadn't been updated since before his father passed on, and most of the rooms had been closed up. "I thought Stoweham House would be ideal."

"A hospital?" The idea refused to sink into his head. He'd seen a hospital once. Dour place, all green walls and strict uniformed matrons. A hospital was the last thing he pictured for Stoweham House.

"Well, more of a convalescent home." She pulled out a newspaper clipping.

"Good Lord," he muttered. "We can't run a convalescent home. We can barely afford to maintain a handful of servants and three family members." Four, if one counted Georgia.

A secret smile played Mother's lips. "That's the beauty of it. If you volunteer your house—"

"Volunteer?"

"—the house, it's the War Office who pays the staff. They provide the supervising officers and the nurses and the servants. They buy the food and fuel. Essentially, they pay for everything that is required to run the place. All you have to sit back and let them."

James paced the room. "Mother, I'm not going to sit back and let anyone do anything. As soon as I'm married, I'm leaving this town and—"

Aunt Violet cried out, "Married?"

Mother, who had been sorting through her folio, paused, her note-filled hands stopping in mid-air.

"What did you say?"

James froze. Uh-oh. Did he say something he shouldn't have? He sorted through his most recent words. "Um…" was the best he could come up with.

Aunt Violet rose to her feet. "Don't tell me you're planning on proposing to that…that…" She waved her hands in the air.

"Eligible young lady?" James finished.

"She's a ghost," finished Aunt Violet in an outburst. "And a most improper one at that."

"It's not her fault she was unclothed." Indignation rose within him. "Besides, she comes from proper family."

"You can't marry a ghost," Aunt Violet insisted.

"She's living now."

"And how long is that going to last?"

James ran his hands through his hair. "For at least another fifty years, God willing." Why was he arguing with his aunt? She had no say in anything to do with his life or the house. No say at all. How had he let her side track him from his original purpose? "Who I marry is entirely up to me. I will marry Georgia."

Mother echoed, "Georgia…?" as if to speak her Christian name was most improper.

Mother might have insisted he call her Miss Palmerton. To him, Georgia was the only bright spark of color in an otherwise bleak existence.

But Aunt Violet wouldn't leave things alone. "How long have you known this…"

"Ghost?"

"Person."

"I've known her my whole life."

Aunt Violet was not amused. "You do not know if

she is suitable."

"Oh, she suits me very well."

She shook her head and rolled her eyes heavenward. "I meant her reputation. After all, we know the Stoweham Ghost wasn't known for her modesty…"

Mother shuffled the papers in her folio. "I've thought about writing a letter to the War Office to offer Stoweham House," she stated loudly.

But James was not letting Aunt Violet's insult slide by. He bent close to murmur in her ear. "Are you casting aspersions on her virtue? Because if you are, I can tell you, beyond a shadow of a doubt, that she was a virgin."

Aunt Violet became very pale and still. James couldn't resist one last parting shot. "I do hope, however, that her virginity isn't a necessary condition for her upcoming marriage."

That got her. She inhaled sharply, her lips pinching tightly.

Before she mustered enough pressure for her outburst, Mother declared, "James Anthony Michael Cowper!" Her hands flutter to her throat. "I… You…" She couldn't finish her sentence.

"I don't care." He backed out of the parlor. "Maybe I should go check her suitability right now."

Mother rose, her hand out in supplication. "Please, James."

He paused, his hand on the door, his back to her. "What?"

"Just…treat her well. Treat her with honor. I know you are not a dishonorable man."

He couldn't meet her eyes at that one.

Mother continued. "If you are going to propose to this…girl, why not a proper courtship? Do everything in the right order. I'm sure I have a suitable ring you could use for an engagement."

His hand remained on the door. He dared not look out into the corridor. "Do you?"

"Unless you wish to get a ring of your own? I thought a family heirloom would be ideal."

"I'm happy with a family heirloom. I assume you have one here in the house?" Mother once kept her nicer jewels in a safe deposit box in a bank in Buckingham. However, since the war began, she'd not been back.

Only now did Aunt Violet find her voice. "Helen, surely you are not considering entertaining this idea."

Mother ignored her. "When were you planning on proposing marriage?"

Was that a slight tremor in her voice?

He turned to her. "Yesterday. Fortunately, she has accepted my offer and the banns are to be read this Sunday."

At this, Mother covered her mouth with both hands while tears filled her eyes.

Aunt Violet let out a sound of disgust. "Of all the foolish—"

"Why the rush?" Mother had found her words. "Aren't you moving a bit, well, fast?"

"I don't have much choice," he countered, his temper rising. "See, the Stoweham Ghost came to me one night with sweet words and soft caresses designed to seduce. I have been compromised and thoroughly ravished by her. Therefore, my reputation is all but in tatters. It is best I marry immediately, or I shall never be able to hold my head up in polite society ever again."

"Now you're being ridiculous," spat Aunt Violet.

James slipped through the door. "Georgia will require your advice in the morning, Mum. She is in need of a proper trousseau. You've only got about three weeks."

Out in the corridor, something thumped against a wall.

"Three weeks?" cried Mother. "Oh, dear. We should start first thing tomorrow morning."

"Can't. Georgia's got far more important things to do."

"Like what?"

"Like me."

On that rather shocking note, he left the parlor, shutting the door a little harder than usual.

There was Georgia, replacing a vase that she must have knocked over. Had she tried walking through the walls again? "Sorry," she apologized. "Habit."

James didn't care. He was too angry. Angry that Mother wouldn't sell the house—not that he needed her permission, but her blessing would have been appreciated. Angry that Aunt Violet cast aspersions on his future bride, and angry that it was taking longer than usual to leave Stoweham for good. He caught Georgia up in his arms and gave her a punishing kiss. He wanted Mother and Aunt Violet to come out and witness just what he wanted to do.

When he released her lips enough to breathe, she gave him a cunning grin. "I believe we have business upstairs?"

Very much so. Without asking, he threw her over

his shoulder and carried her upwards.

He heard the parlor door open behind him. His two relatives gasped together.

"James," Mother called out. "Put her down!"

He refused to justify that with a reply, never mind compliance.

Georgia, however, had no compunction. "See you in the morning!" she called out to the fretting women.

Let them fret. Let them worry, let them wonder. The only person whose opinion mattered was in his arms and very willing.

He had no problems with getting the bedroom door open. Once in the bedroom, he slammed it shut with his foot. Oh, he hoped they'd heard that.

For a moment, he considered throwing Georgia on the bed, but that might be too much. He set her carefully on her feet. But the moment she was out of his arms, he pulled her in and kissed her hard again.

"Are you taking me because you're angry at your family?" she asked when he moved to suck on her neck.

James paused as guilt crept up his spine. He pulled back. "I..." What could he say?

She laid a finger over his lips. "I don't mind." Her hands tore at the buttons of his waistcoat. "If this is how you behave when you get angry, I am all for it."

He looked at her, momentarily stunned, while she couldn't get his coat off fast enough.

"I'm so happy you're a man of passion," she said. His shirt lost a few buttons when her impatience overcame her dexterity. "I've seen far too many men who would hit a woman if he was angry. Or he'd yell at her. Or worse, give her the silent treatment and ignore her, seeking his comfort elsewhere." She'd had him half-undressed at this point, snagging his undershirt up and over his head. "But you, if you are ever angry, or happy or sad or frustrated, if this is how you reply, I approve."

She'd freed his belt. The feeling of her hands on his trouser buttons stirred him. Before he could move, she'd pushed him to the bed and had climbed on top. Her clothes were in the way. He helped her as they undid all those tiny little buttons that kept her blouse closed. So many clothes, he wanted to rip them off.

"Tell me. What is the worst—" No, that wasn't the best description. "I mean, what is the strangest, the most shocking practice you've ever seen between a couple?"

She whispered it in his ear, just as she discarded her skirt. Mouths weren't only for kissing, apparently. He looked at her as what she had asked sank in. Then he looked to her nether region. Really? One could do that?

He thought back to the morning. Yes, Georgia had done to him what she proposed he do for her. The memory of her lips along his shaft, taking him into her mouth had quite surprised him. She'd given him no warning at the time, merely slid down and licked his hard maleness. Never in his imagining, certainly not in the whispered tales adolescent boys shared, had anyone ever mentioned this particular technique. "I say," he had declared at the time, intending to protest her actions. But it had felt so good. He had let her do whatever she wanted.

The thought of him returning the favor thrilled and appalled him. What would Mother say if she knew? What would Aunt Violet say? She'd be shocked to her bones.

By gum, he would do it.

James had Georgia sprawled on the bed before she could remove her shift. He bent down and applied his lips to the other pair of lips he'd never imagined kissing. That's what this was like, a deep, passionate kiss. She tasted salty, and not entirely unpleasant. His knowledge of her anatomy was rather limited and new, with his only experience when she had showed him what to do with his fingers.

But this was different, better, more intimate. He found one particular little bud, almost like a little tongue. He ran his own tongue over it, to spectacular results. Georgia bucked up and cried out in pleasure.

Oh yes, he thought. Let them hear you and wonder. Thus he plied her until her voice was little more than ragged gasps.

He couldn't stand it anymore. He had to take her before he embarrassed himself. Sliding up her body, he plunged into her moist center, burying himself in the soft, tight sweetness of her vagina. Her hands clutched his buttocks and drove him deeper. She wanted it? She could have it. James gave himself over to his instinct and rode her hard. He gave voice to his own arrival, only a moment after hers. After, they lay there panting together, Georgia's pleasure evident on her face. How could a smile be so broad yet look so relaxed at the same time?

James rose. The light needed turning out. He sat on the edge of the bed, his head in his hands. "I'm sorry. I should never have done that."

Georgia sat up, the bedclothes sliding off her form. "Don't you ever apologize. Ever." She slid her arms about his waist and laid her chin on his shoulder. "I know you better than you think." She nudged a kiss onto his skin. "Trust me, if this is how you take out your frustrations, I have no objection. None at all."

He laid his head alongside hers. "I wouldn't know. You are my first," he confessed.

"And I certainly hope to be your last."

That suited him fine. "Still, what happens when..." Images of the future, of reality, intruded on the rosy little world he'd been living in the past couple of days.

"When we become an old, married couple?"

No. That sounded delightful. "What happens when you're not in the mood? What happens when I—" He shook his head. "It's one thing to be angry. It's another to force myself on someone who doesn't wish my attention. What happens if I don't choose respect over anger?"

She pressed her face into his neck before she answered. "James, I am not like other women. While my body is still young, I have more than a lifetime of knowledge. I also have an insight into what it means to be mortal. I promise I will always be there for you. Sometimes I think you mortals take yourselves for granted. Your bodies are all you know. You don't realize what a gift and a joy than can be. For you, pain is to be avoided. I know of the housewives who have wearied of their husband's physical attention. I've heard their conversations, where they stand off to the side and scheme of ways to avoid warm beds. But me, I spent far too long unable to touch, unable to taste. I marvel that range of experiences our bodies let us have. So what if one feels hunger? It means the body is craving food. I rejoice when I feel pain as well as pleasure, because it means I'm truly alive once more."

James stiffened. "I didn't hurt you, have I? That's the last thing I want." His insides sank. "Truly, I am sorry. I should have been more gentle with you."

"Why? You needed me. And I was happy to be needed. Promise to love me always, and I will always be there for you."

He nodded, in spite of the guilt in his heart.

Georgia nudged him once more. "Consider this. What happens if I am angry? Would you consider turning me away?"

"Never."

"There you go. Now put out the light, come to bed, snuggle up to me, and let us sleep. We have much to do tomorrow, especially if we are going up in battle against a pair of women who do not have the same outlet for their frustrations as we have."

He did as he was bade. Tonight James settled into Georgia's arms. She said nothing for the rest of the night but held him close and stroked his wavy hair. Here was someone who had always watched over him, who cared for him, who tolerated his earlier temper tantrum and who had reassured him that everything would be all right.

He had missed that. How long had it been since someone else shouldered his emotional burden? How long had it been since he had someone he could talk to in confidence? Had he ever had anyone like that? He couldn't recall.

That night he vowed to himself to do whatever it took to keep Georgia happy and in his life.

Chapter 7
Making Peace

His future bride was not the only lady in his life he needed to keep happy. The one who gave him that life also deserved his respect.

In the early hours of the morning, as the household stirred for the day, James slipped out from under Georgia's protective arms and wrapped himself in his dressing gown. Then he padded down the hallway to stand by Mother's door.

In the wake of his father's death, certain budgetary cuts had to be made. Valets and lady's maids were among the first to go. James had grown used to clothing himself but Mother never truly got accustomed to a lack of personal servant. Thus, Mother and Aunt Violet made do in assisting each other to dress. Another consequence of no personal servants was that Mother no longer lay abed in the mornings, awaiting breakfast on a tray.

Thus, he waited. He knew when she rose. He had not long to wait. Her door creaked open, and she came out, hair askew and a heaviness to her step.

He felt a tug of guilt. "Good morning, Mum."

She looked up at him with sad eyes. He dropped his gaze. "I'm so sorry," he muttered. "I never intended to hurt you."

She folded her arms. "Well, you did."

"I know." And he honestly didn't know how to make it any better. "Still, my behavior was inexcusable."

Silence lay between them for several moments.

"And what about poor Miss Palmerton? Your actions toward her were not exactly stellar."

"I have done nothing toward her that she did not specifically request of me." The thought of his face buried between her limbs last night brought a blush to his face. He almost could not admit to himself how much he'd enjoyed that. What other skills did his future wife have in her repertoire?

"Really? Did she request that you carry her upstairs in that shocking manner? Did you..." her voice dropped low, "did you compromise her?"

That touched upon last night's sore spot. "Funny how you aren't worried about me being compromised."

She waved a hand. "You're a man. You can take care of yourself. But what about her? She has no family, no friends to stand up for her."

Now he did meet Mother's eyes. "That's because we are her family. I will be her husband in a very short time. That means you will be her mother-in-law and a rather necessary figure in her life. She is well-acquainted with everyone from the village, though I could not call them her friends, nor mine, come to think of it."

Mother took this in, a fretful look on her face. "Still, what about her reputation?"

"I honestly don't know. I ask that you not mention it again. I do not know if anyone in the village has recognized her as the Stoweham Ghost. If they have, then her reputation is what it is, and the question of her virtue will have no impact. That is what you must worry about. I have no plans to abandon her, so the question of her virtue is null." It wasn't so much that a young lady's reputation was virtuous that raised questions as to whether or not her belly would swell with child. Their marriage would come soon enough to make that a moot point.

"So you intend to go through with this marriage?"

"I do." Very much so.

"Are the banns being read today?"

Today? "Is it Sunday?"

"Aye. And I do expect you to attend church. Both of you."

Oh, now there was a prospect he'd completely forgotten. Yes, he'd been a dutiful parishioner, attending Vicar Johnson's tedious services with Mother and Aunt Violet every Sunday. The rest of the village would be there.

That did put him in a sticky spot. James would have liked nothing more than to avoid them for the next three weeks. However, if his banns were read out in church and he wasn't there, surely the gossips' tongues would run riot.

He sighed. "Yes, we'll be there." Oh, dear. Slight problem. "But what will Georgia wear?"

"I really wish you'd call her Miss Palmerton. At least put on the semblance of propriety."

"Now you sound like Aunt Violet."

Mother humphed at that. "And what about Aunt Violet? You said some beastly things to her as well."

"Not quite ready to be sorry for that yet." He refused to give up his stubborn streak. She might stand on the higher moral ground and consider it her right to lecture, but where had that standing gotten her in life? What old maid truly enjoyed her solitude? Sometimes following the rules and doing what was right were two different things.

That did not impress Mother. Instead, she changed the subject. "I suppose your sister's old wardrobe will have to do until we can visit a decent modiste, though Joan was bigger boned."

Nothing that couldn't be taken up or let out. Was Georgia clever with a needle? Mother could do embroidery, as any gently bred lady could, but when it came to semptstressing, that was another matter entirely.

Her eyes lit up. "Oh, and we'll have to figure out some sort of wedding dress. I hope she is not a proud lady, for there is not enough time to get anything proper made up. Alas, anything of your sister's is well and truly out of fashion."

Georgia probably wouldn't care. "I'll ask her."

He pushed off the wall. He would fetch his sister's trunks from the attic and let Georgia have full rein of their contents.

"Also," Mother said, grabbing his arm as he made to leave, "you will need a ring. If one is to look properly engaged, you will need a ring." With this, she hastened into her bedroom. Soon she emerged, several rings hooked on her fingers. "These are too small for my fingers now, but once, when I was young, I wore them with ease." She sighed over the matronly pudginess that had overcome her in her middle age. "How about this nice sapphire one?"

James shuddered. That one was too much like the cold silver ring that rested in his waistcoat pocket. He'd have to have a word with Georgia regarding what they did with that one. Until they came to a decision he kept it close, lest it come to mischief.

He looked over Mother's offerings. Most of them were silver, the precious metal used most by debutantes and young ladies. Despite her appearance, Georgia was none of those. On Mother's smallest finger was a tiny gold ring plain in design and set with four different colored stones.

"That one," he said.

Mother blinked at him. "Really? But it's so small."

It looked nothing like the cursed ring Georgia had worn for a century. Also, of all the rings, it was the most likely to fit her delicate hands. "It's perfect."

She slipped it off and handed it over, apparently displeased by his selection. If she didn't want him to have it, why did she include it in the offerings?

"What are the stones?" he asked.

She took it back, and held it at arm's length for focus. "A diamond, I believe, emerald, amethyst and possibly a ruby?" She handed it to him.

He nodded. "It will do."

Slipping it over the first knuckle of his pinkie, he gave his mother a spontaneous kiss on the cheek. "Thanks, Mum."

She put her hand over the kissed cheek, a gently bemused look on her face.

"Give us an hour," he said. "We'll come to church with you."

Let the gossips have their day. If they were to talk, let it be about what he had done, and not what he had failed to do.

****

James had made it down the attic steps unaided with his sister Joan's trunks. He never thought he'd be grateful for anything she'd left behind after her marriage. Georgia, clad only in yesterday's shift, had taken great joy in the contents, declaring them splendid enough. As she sorted through for something suitable, James informed her that it was Sunday and their attendance at church was required.

"I suppose so," she replied, lifting a filmy summer frock with a low, round neck. "This might do, though I suspect it would need a corset." She dug through the trunk, separating clothes into various piles. "Ah," she cried in delight as she lifted something corset-like out of the collection. "That looks familiar."

James shaded his eyes from the sight of what she called a brassiere. It looked like a corset, as it laced on the sides, but did not extend to the hips. Georgia found a few other things while James devoutly kept his eyes averted. Georgia had a good laugh at that.

"If we are going to church, we should bathe, having forgotten last night."

Fair enough. Mother had finished with the bathroom for the morning and Aunt Violet had not yet risen. Or perhaps she was avoiding them?

"Shall I go first, or you?" James offered.

There was that wicked gleam in her eye again. "Who said we had to bathe alone?"

****

James had only ever bathed alone. To have Georgia in the tub with him, lying back against his body, was quite the experience, especially for something so every day as bathing. It seemed so much more pleasant to run a soapy flannel over someone else. He looked forward

118

to repeating the experience soon.

"What is this?" she asked, inspecting his hand.

Ah, the ring. "That's for you, if you'll have it. Or rather, that's for you if you'll have me."

"An engagement ring?" With gentle fingers, she eased it off his soapy hand.

"Mm hmm. I thought you'd appreciate a ring that means life, rather than death."

She said nothing to that, but held the ring, studying it. Georgia's death ring had been on her right hand. An engagement ring went on the left.

"May I think about it?" she eventually said. "The ring, I mean. Absolutely I am marrying you, but..."

"I understand." He took the ring back, replacing it on his finger. "Speaking of rings, I still have the other one. I didn't know what you wanted done with it."

"We need to get rid of it. I never want to see it again."

He sighed. "I thought about throwing it in a river or something."

But she refused that idea. "We can't risk it ever being found. It's too dangerous. We need to find a jeweller to melt it down."

Stoweham had none, and it wouldn't be until after the wedding that they would be somewhere else. "I'll keep it safe until then."

The doorknob rattled, followed by the defeated sigh of Aunt Violet. "James, is that you in there."

"We'll be out soon," Georgia called back.

No reply, then a muttered, "Oh, for the love of..."

James couldn't help but smile at the angry sound of his aunt's retreating footsteps. "Really, we shouldn't antagonize her."

"Probably not," Georgia replied, her words holding no promise.

****

While Aunt Violet might disapprove, Mother found Georgia's outfit entirely suitable for church. The brassiere thing pulled Georgia's round bosom in enough to keep the light blouse from looking like a stuffed sausage. The plain brown skirt, being of a wider cut, fit well over her hips. The matching jacket settled nicely on her shoulders, even if the sleeves needed rolling up.

"If you don't mind," Mother said, "I'd like to take the long way around. I have some things I'd like to discuss."

James groaned. Was he to be subject to another lecture?

But no. Mother started off by saying, "I've written to the War Office and to Royal Bucks offering Stoweham House as a convalescent home. Well, the letters will go out tomorrow."

They set off down the drive, James and Georgia arm-in-arm, with Mother on his other side. Aunt Violet kept pace with Mother, saying nothing, but shooting disapproving glances James-ward. The morning was lovely, with sun peeking through the clouds, though it promised rain later.

"I figured, either they will accept our offer or they will not. If they don't, we could rent out Stoweham House, either in its entirety, or by the room. And should that not work," Mother drew a deep breath, "then we can sell the house."

Aunt Violet made a noise of protest.

"I doubt it will come to that," Mother said. "If one

can believe the papers, there are plenty of soldiers who need to convalesce in the country."

James still hadn't had a chance to read the paper, or what was left of it, if Mother had clipped out all articles of interest. He had to admit her plan had merit. If he had sold Stoweham House without trying other avenues first, Aunt Violet would never let him live it down. Who knew what cousin Reggie would say, not that he ever came to visit often enough to miss the place. He had no desire to keep the house, much less live in it, so having someone foot the bill for its everyday running sounded like a fair compromise.

He gave Mother's arm a squeeze. "I'm happy to let you try this. But please understand, as soon as we are married, Georgia and I will be leaving Stoweham for good."

Mother nodded. "Whatever you think is best. Though I wish I could convince you to stay."

When he refused to have anything more to say on the subject, Mother engaged Georgia in discussions of wedding plans.

Now that he thought about it, it was probably the longest and best conversation the two most important women in his life had ever had.

****

Before long, the Cowpers arrived to church. Other Stoweham families also walked in for their weekly devotions. Some stood in clumps in the churchyard catching up on gossip and other news. No wonder Georgia was able to know who's who and what's what in Stoweham. Sunday must have been her most favorite day of the week.

He looked at her, with her arm tucked into his. Her

gaze roamed about, but the tightness of her grip betrayed her nerves.

He patted her hand. "It'll be all right."

"Easy for you to say," she replied. "This is the first time they've seen me with clothes on."

As they approached, several pairs of eyes turned their way. Tongues ceased wagging as people stared at James Cowper and the strange young lady accompanying him. James was used to the stares and the cold shoulders. Georgia was not.

Still, she comported herself admirably. As they passed within speaking distance, she'd nod her head and greet them by name. Mr. and Mrs. Jones, the Cooper family, the Rameys. She even had a word for Ethel Forsythe, attending without her husband Billy. It was a cool and distant greeting, which Ethel replied with narrowed eyes. One thing to be said for Georgia, she did have manners.

As they entered the chapel, soft organ music greeted them. The Cowper family had always enjoyed the front pew at St. Mary's, having contributed much to the chapel's repair and upkeep. As they sat in their customary spot, James resisted looking behind him. The back of his head itched with the thought of a hundred stares bearing down on it. Georgia sat next to him, eyes forward, waiting for the service to begin, her hand tight in his.

The organ notes faded away and everyone rose as the procession began. When Vicar Johnson noticed them in the pew, a slight frown creased his brow. Georgia smiled and gave him a little wave. But the moment he diverted his gaze, she resumed her tense grip on James' hand.

He kept his focus on the service and held on to Georgia's hands. The sound of worship echoed through the chapel, the sonorous tones of the vicar, the shuffle of feet as everyone rose for hymns, the sound of many out-of-tune voices against the organ, the emptiness of silence for meditation. James closed his eyes and let it wash over him.

At the end of the second Lesson came the time for the reading of the banns.

Vicar Johnson, at the lectern, shuffled his notes and cleared his throat a few times. He drew a shuddery breath and closed his eyes for a moment. Then he began, "I publish the banns of marriage between James Anthony Michael Cowper of Stoweham and the Honorable Miss Georgia Mary Palmerton of...of Stoweham."

At this, the congregation broke out in murmuring.

"This is the first time of asking. If any of you know cause or just impediment why these two persons should not be joined together in Holy Matrimony, ye are to declare it." Then he paused, as if fully expecting a response.

However, Mother had turned to face the congregation expectantly. She sat there, staring them all down, daring them to utter a peep.

James risked a glance. Nobody said anything, though plenty of heads were bent together. Had the news stunned them all, or were they trying to figure out who Georgia was?

At least Vicar Johnson had not declared her the Stoweham Ghost. That would have turned the congregation upside down. When James looked back to Georgia, he saw her gaze fixed firmly on Vicar

Johnson, a smug little smile on her lips. He needn't have worried about her. She knew Vicar Johnson sufficiently—held enough of his secrets—to ensure his compliance.

Nobody had raised any objections. One bann down, two more to go.

Unlike other Sundays, Mother did not stay to speak with the other ladies of the parish. She and Aunt Violet agreed that perhaps it was best they return home, Mother's weak excuse being they had much preparation before the wedding. The parishioners watched them pass.

Georgia clung to his arm. "I don't like their eyes," she muttered to him.

He agreed. Something wasn't sitting right. Surely they couldn't object to his getting married.

Or were they remembering a few nights ago when he'd embarrassed Billy Forsythe and reclaimed his Silver War Badge? He looked at their cold, distant faces. How many of them were in the pub that night?

Mrs. Bathurst, one of the more prominent ladies of the community rushed up to Mother, even going so far as to grab her by the arm. "A word, if I may, Mrs. Cowper?"

Mother may have been one of the highest ranking ladies in Stoweham, but Mrs. Bathurst was one of the most influential. A few of Mrs. Bathurst's supporters followed, vainly trying not to let their rampant curiosity overcome their dignity.

"Please, I pray, introduce me to your future daughter-in-law," Mrs. Bathurst said.

Mother was at a loss for words when Mrs. Bathurst addressed Georgia directly. "Are you newly come to

Stoweham?"

Georgia didn't miss a beat. "No, Mrs. Bathurst, I've been here for years. I remember when your lad Johnny fell off that very wall." She pointed to the low stone wall surrounding the church. "He broke his arm and you had to take him all the way into Buckingham because Doctor Stone had gone to visit his sister that week."

Now Mrs. Bathurst was at a loss for words.

Mother, her discomfort showing in the trembling of her hands, took Georgia by the arm and drew her away. "We have much to do, my dear."

But the ladies wouldn't let her go that fast. James had been all but shoved back by a disapproving Aunt Violet. Would they never get free and through the gate?

Mrs. Amherst, a younger yet bossy matron. "If you live here, why have we not seen you at the Women's Auxiliary meetings?"

Georgia was good. She laid a hand over her bosom and replied, "You mean, like the last one, when Maisie Fredericks spilt punch down her best blouse?"

Mrs. Amherst blinked. "But surely you weren't there. How did you know?"

Georgia hadn't been there. James knew that for sure. The Community Hall where the Women's Auxiliary met had been well outside of her ghostly range.

"Everyone there saw what happened. That's why she missed the Church Floral Committee. Poor dear only has the one good blouse."

At this, the other ladies looked away in embarrassment. One did not speak of the privations war had brought. Everyone was expected to do their part, whether investing in War Loans or donating to the Red Cross. It was patriotic to appear not able to afford luxuries. Poor Mrs. Fredericks, her husband still off at war, had not been able to afford much.

Georgia laid a hand on Mrs. Amherst's arm. "By the way, I'm glad you decided against amaryllis for the chapel for next week. I have grown rather tired of them every service."

With that, she took James' arm. He tipped his hat to the bemused ladies. Together, he and Georgia hurried out of the churchyard as quickly as their dignity could take them.

****

The next morning, Mother and Georgia put yesterday's discussed plans into action. Georgia needed the trappings of life, and that included a new trousseau. Aunt Violet was volunteered to go into town on a shopping expedition, armed with a list of needful things for Georgia and a few letters from Mother for posting.

"How are you with a needle?" Mother asked Georgia as they dug through the trunks James had brought down to the spare bedroom. Although she'd accepted James' and Georgia's sinful ways, she still insisted that Georgia needed a room of her own.

"I have a fair hand with embroidery and general mending." Georgia held up the over-frilly blouses. "I don't know about remaking clothes, though."

Mother shooed James out.

And fair enough. He had his own life to sort out and pack. As soon as they were married, he and Georgia were hopping on the next train out of Buckingham. They would lose themselves in the smoky anonymity of London, and didn't that sound delightful?

He ransacked his bedroom for anything he wished to take with him. Other than clothes and a shaving kit, there really wasn't much he wanted, no childhood mementoes or favorite toys or treasured letters.

His gaze fell to the cursed ring on the bureau. He picked it up and rolled it about his fingers. Here was something they dared not leave behind. But what were they to do with it? Melt it down, possibly? Would fire destroy the curse?

As he played with it, he carelessly slipped it over the tip of his finger. When that happened, the whole world went black.

James opened his eyes and sat up. He felt much lighter. He didn't feel much of anything at all. The ring was no longer on his hand.

His pale incorporeal hand.

With growing dread, he turned around to see his body slumped on the floor, the ring still snugly up against his first knuckle. Sure, it was futile, but he couldn't help reaching for the ring. His spirit hand passed through his physical hand with no effect. Another cold thought occurred to him. As he looked at his ghostly self, his embarrassment grew. He, like Georgia before him, was completely naked.

Oops.

Movement was fairly simple. While his legs moved in semblance of walking, he didn't need to do this to actually move. With just a thought he could glide across the floor and through the closed door.

Pausing outside Georgia's room he called out, "Georgia?"

"You can't come in, James," she replied.

Not that he wanted to. He certainly didn't want

Mother to see him like this. "That's all right. I need you to come help me with something."

Mother called out, "Does it have to be right now?"

At first he wanted to say yes. However, upon further reflection, if he sounded urgent, they both might come running out. That's not something he wanted. "Not right now, but I'd prefer sooner, rather than later. I'll be in the bedroom." Eventually Georgia would find him and she would know what to do. What was a few more minutes? She had waited a century.

As he drifted down the corridor, he heard the door open behind him. "Oh, goodness gracious!" Georgia exclaimed.

James turned around to see Georgia in the corridor with her eyes wide and both hands clamped over her mouth.

"Is something wrong?" Mother called out.

James had barely enough time to leap into the wall as Mother came out of the bedroom.

Now that was a strange sensation. He flinched as he went through the wall, though he didn't feel a thing. He saw the wooden beams as he passed through, and then he was in another room. He heard Mother's and Georgia's muffled voices, but couldn't make out their words. Best he returned to the bedroom and his body.

Moments later Georgia entered the room. When she saw his fallen body, she cried out and dashed over. Quickly she pulled the ring off his finger and flung it across the room.

Everything went dark.

James drew a needful breath. He opened his eyes to find himself back in his body and his face muffled against Georgia's bosom.

Her body shook as she sobbed. "Why would you do that?"

"I'm sorry," he answered as soon as he could get his head free. "It was an accident."

She pulled back. Her eyes were angry and frightened as she shook him. "Never do that again."

He gathered her into his arms. "I won't."

They agreed the ring was too dangerous to leave lying about. James stuck it in his waistcoat pocket which Georgia stitched shut with a needle she produced from the pincushion in her pocket.

"There," she said, as she snipped the thread. "Now no one will be tempted."

Still, it was quite some time before they were willing to let go of each other. Even when Mother appeared and questioned them, they would not let go.

Sunday could not come soon enough.

Chapter 8
The Wedding

The day of their wedding delivered on its promise of rain.

Mother peered out from between the parlor curtains at all the water falling from the skies. "Such a terrible omen," she moaned. "It is as if the Good Lord himself refuses to let you have a nice day."

James remained by the fire, warming his hands. Georgia's ring was still on his pinkie, where it would stay until the service. He'd tried to convince her to put it on, but she refused.

"I'll wear a ring for the wedding ceremony, but after that…"

So he kept it. As he studied it, he wondered; he could get it resized to fit his ring finger instead? The other ring had been transferred to his Morning Gray waistcoat pocket. He didn't have a needle and thread, so he hoped it would remain secure until they could reach London.

Georgia joined Mother at the window. "I suppose we'll have to adapt our plans."

Mother sighed. "I tried and tried to borrow a carriage, but no one would agree. At this point, I would have been happy with a wagon. Oh, your lovely gown will be positively spoiled." She sniffed. "After all that hard work."

Georgia's head tilted to the side. "Only if I wear it."

Mother stiffened. "You will not go back to your ghostly ways. I will not have you parading about Stoweham without a stitch—"

"I meant what if I only wore it inside the chapel? I know we planned on returning here after service to change, but perhaps it would be better to take the gown with us and change there? That way we do not have to worry about rain or mud or anything spoiling it."

James sat up. "I think that's a splendid idea." His original plan had been to wear a simple frock coat over his Morning Grays to church and change into his morning coat for the wedding, while awaiting Georgia and Mother. Also, if Cook's reports of village rumors were anything to go by, if he was not there to escort Georgia, she could very well have been the victim of gawping spectators, or worse. Seems enough people were not happy that James was getting married. Perhaps it was best she change at the chapel. It's not like they would be ruining any traditions.

Procession and pomp had been all but abandoned. Indeed, most of the usual trappings of a wedding were missing, from flowers to guests. While Mother fretted over such a simple ceremony, James and Georgia believed it best. What else mattered other than the ceremony?

Nevertheless, Georgia and Mother went upstairs to pack the wedding gown, which James was still not allowed to see, into a Gladstone bag. Then the Cowpers and one Cowper-to-be set off in the downpour to stake an early claim to the chapel, in a parade of mackintoshes and wellies.

The attendance at services that morning was no more and no less than usual in spite of the weather.

Once again Vicar Johnson read the banns. "This is the third and last time of asking."

Yes, there were the usual murmurs, but no one raised a protest. James watched as a satisfied smile settled on Georgia's face. They'd done it. No one had offered objection to their wedding. She gave his hand an excited squeeze.

He had no idea what was said the rest of the service, or indeed hadn't noticed when it ended. All he could do was hold Georgia's hand.

The chapel cleared quicker than usual thanks to the rain. Vicar Johnson, who had been farewelling parishioners on the cold, damp porch, soon returned.

James rose. Georgia and Mother disappeared with their Gladstone to who-knew-where. Aunt Violet simply sank onto the pew, arms folded, lost in her thoughts. The darkness of the clouds outside dimmed the noontime light until it resembled twilight. The rain continued to patter on the roof, a gentle, rolling sound. The chapel took on a gentle light as the assistant curate lit the lamps one by one.

"Vicar Johnson," James said. "Could we move the wedding up?"

Vicar Johnson, who had been huffing his way up the aisle, paused. "No," he replied.

That took James aback. "May I ask why?"

The vicar stared at James as if he'd sprouted flowers on his forehead. "What about your guests?"

"We have none," he admitted. "And if the villagers were to show up, you know it would be from sheer curiosity and not from genuine sentiment."

Vicar Johnson pursed his lips as he considered. "Does the bride agree to this?"

It was Aunt Violet who spoke. "I dare say she would. Miss Palmerton has not been one for patience."

Still, Vicar Johnson wasn't fully convinced. "This is highly irregular."

James spread his arms. "This is a time of war. Nothing is regular."

By the time all the lamps of the chapel were lit, giving the chapel a warm glow, Mother came out. "She's ready. Now we wait."

James, who had returned to the pew, rose once more. "We're not waiting."

Mother's hands flapped. "But the wedding is not until one."

"And?"

Mother's voice dropped. "I thought you wanted to do things properly."

James took his groom's place at the altar. Vicar Johnson had gone to fetch the parish book to record the wedding. "I am. But we have no reason to wait an extra half hour. My bride is ready now, and I'm sure Vicar Johnson would appreciate getting home a bit early for luncheon."

Mother acquiesced.

The vicar returned, several books in hand. Two he left on the lectern, the third, his Common Book of Prayer, he brought forth. "Let us begin."

Mother hastened off to fetch Georgia. The sound of the rain increased on the roof. How wise it had been not to go home to change. How sad it was that there was no carriage to deliver them back. Naturally, no other guests showed up, the rain being heavy enough to wash away any curiosity. With no music but the rain, James turned to await his bride.

Out of the ethereal light of the chapel, a white figure drifted, silent and graceful as Georgia Palmerton slid into view. A gown of exquisite shaping clung to her body, accentuating her gentle curves. Mother's diadem reposed on her curls and a full veil of bobbinet encased her form, making her look more ghostly than ever. She moved with purpose, not lingering.

James' breath caught in his throat. Could there be any lovelier creature on earth, living or dead? Even Vicar Johnson let out a small noise.

Georgia glided up to him, a smile of delight on her face. Behind them, Mother and Aunt Violet came to stand.

James reached out to take Georgia's eager hands, only to have them batted back by the vicar.

"Not yet," Vicar Johnson chided. The ceremony began. "Dearly beloved, we are gathered together here in the sight of God to join together this man and this woman in holy matrimony."

James looked at Georgia. A warmth of joy filled him. He would never be alone again.

Likewise, Georgia's eyes lit up. She clutched her hands together to keep them from reaching out for him. There would be plenty of time for that later, and for all the rest of the days of their lives.

Vicar Johnson's words flowed over him, and he couldn't remember half of them. "First, it was ordained for the procreation of children," the vicar said.

Of course. He may have been untitled, but he was still gentry, and the next generation was expected of him. How comforting. He would have children.

Georgia's children.

"Secondly, it was ordained for a remedy against sin, and to avoid fornication…"

At least Georgia had the sense to look abashed. James couldn't stop the grin that spread across his face. It was good to be wanted and loved.

"Thirdly, It was ordained for the mutual society, help, and comfort, that the one ought to have of the other…"

Absolutely. Georgia filled his life like no other. The thought of her calmed his heart. Her presence stirred him up. Life would never be dull or lonely with Georgia.

"James Anthony Michael Cowper," said Vicar Johnson, startling him.

"What?"

Georgia gave a small laugh.

"Wilt thou have this woman to thy wedded wife?"

His face flushed. Of course he would.

"Georgia Mary Palmerton, wilt thou have this man to thy wedded husband?"

All he could see was the light of life in Georgia's eyes.

She replied, "I will."

"Who giveth this woman to be married to this man?"

Ah. A very good question, one that caught James by surprise. Georgia, likewise, hadn't anticipated it.

Unexpectedly, it was Aunt Violet who stood up. "I do, in place of her father, who is dead."

Vicar Johnson accepted this. To James, he said, "Now, you can take her hand."

Her grip was firm and comforting. James

marvelled at the warmth her fingers gave him. He repeated his vows. A gentle tap on his hand from the vicar's book prompted him to release it.

The vicar spoke to Georgia. "Now take James by the right hand."

She did and she repeated her vows. "...I give thee my troth."

Vicar Johnson asked, "Do you have the ring?"

The ring. Little rivulets of fear ran through him. The light went out of Georgia's countenance as worry crossed her face. James put his hand over his waistcoat pocket. How did Vicar Johnson know? The sound of rain increased. His heart beat also increased and he feared spots appearing before his eyes. But Georgia shook her head. She gestured to his right hand.

Of course. On his pinkie was the four-stoned ring she refused to wear earlier. With a little effort he removed it and placed it on the book. The fear bled away, but Georgia still looked concerned.

Vicar Johnson handed the ring back to James. "Place and hold the ring on her finger."

Georgia raised a trembling hand. James took it, but didn't slip the ring on just yet. "I promise," he whispered. "Everything will be fine."

She nodded, though the tension hadn't left her.

James slid the ring over the first knuckle and held it there.

Nothing happened. Georgia, still very much alive, let out a sigh.

"With this ring I thee wed," said James. "With my body I thee worship." He couldn't help but smile at this.

Her eyes softened.

"And with all my worldly goods I thee endow. In

the Name of the Father, and of the Son, and of the Holy Ghost. Amen." He slid the ring all the way onto her finger before gathering up her hands into his.

They'd done it. They were married. As they knelt down before the vicar for the final prayer, James whispered, "You can take it off after the ceremony if you wish. I don't mind."

She gave him a grateful nod.

Vicar Johnson pronounced them husband and wife. As he turned to the Lord's Table, Georgia leaned over and, not bothering to remove her veil, kissed James as the sound of the rain enveloped them. The sound of Vicar Johnson singing the psalm were all but lost in the echo of the chapel.

A loud noise, very much like gunshot, startled James. He pulled away from Georgia. She followed, her hand on his arm, her eyes full of concern.

"Lookee here, boys!" called out an unwelcome voice. Billy Forsythe. "Looks like we're just in time for a wedding."

James spun around as his heart turned to ice. Billy strode up the aisle, followed by four other men, none of them too steady on their feet. Drunk, on a Sunday afternoon? Drunk men were never up to any good. They did not carry weapons, but one pulled unsuccessfully at the stopper of a large jug. Another held a burlap sack. On the outside were several bits of fluff, as if they'd come from a henhouse.

Feathers. The sack was full of feathers.

His gaze darted to the jug. At first he thought it might be alcohol, but the lid was too large. Surely not tar.

His heart thumped hard. They would dare tar and

feather him on his wedding day?

Vicar Johnson, startled, rose to his feet. "This is a house of the Lord."

Billy ignored him. He grabbed James by the lapels. Georgia tugged uselessly on Billy's arm.

"See here," said Billy, his reddened nose inches from James'. "I object to this wedding on account o' the bride isn't a real person. She's a ghost. You can't marry a ghost." He leaned over to Georgia, a look of covetousness on his face. "Besides. I know she ain't virtuous."

At this, Georgia's jaw dropped. "I beg your pardon!"

Billy laughed. "You've been a right old tease, haven't you, my little ghostie? Flaunting your naked body to all the men. Oh, it took me a while to figure out who you were, but I figgered it out in the end."

The others behind him nodded, all but the one who couldn't unstopper the jug. His hands couldn't get purchase on the wet crockery.

James glanced over to Mother, but she was gone. He hoped she'd gone for help. But Aunt Violet was there, her face white with anger, fists clenched.

The jug slipped out of the man's hands, to break on the floor. A sticky brown goo oozed out.

What was that? Molasses?

"See," taunted Billy. "We always thought you a phantom, with no physical form at all. Yet here we see you in the flesh." He looked her up and down. "Had I known you could do this, I would have let you part your pretty little legs for me long ago."

James attempted to knee Billy in the groin and got himself thrown to the ground for his efforts. Billy gave him a kick to his ribs for his troubles. Hot pain shot through James' torso. The cursed ring fell out of James' pocket, to clatter loudly across the floor.

Georgia cried out, "Oh, James, the ring!"

Everyone's gaze followed the ring as it rolled across the stone floor to bump up against the leg of a pew.

Billy blinked. "What have we here?" He picked it up, studying it.

James pushed himself up from the floor. His right knee ached from the impact, as did his ribs. "That ring is the secret to the Stoweham Ghost."

"James, no!" Georgia's eyes filled with tears and she pressed her trembling hands to her face.

He continued. "The Stoweham Ghost is solid and real to whoever possesses that ring."

Billy clenched the ring his fist. "Now she belongs to me!"

Georgia retreated behind James.

"Not yet," James said to Billy. "You have to wear the ring."

Billy lifted the ring closer to his face. In his clumsy, one-handed way, he fumbled the ring about until he could slip it over his finger. The lights flickered. Without any warning, Billy dropped to the floor.

Georgia flung her arms about James. He gathered her up and they retreated.

The feather bearer overcame his surprise and crept forward. "Billy? You all right?"

Everyone held their breath as they watched the fallen body.

Suddenly, Billy's ghost sat up. "What happened?"

he muttered, as he studied his ethereal hands. Then he saw his body on the floor. "What did you do to me?" he cried. He spun around, but the two men behind him darted back.

He moved forward toward James, but James stood his ground. A ghost could not hurt him.

The ghost of Billy flowed around the chapel, chasing the men and causing Vicar Johnson to cover his head with his arms. The young assistant curate and Mother clung to each other in fear. All the men, their courage gone, fled the chapel.

Billy's distressed ghost chased after them, calling, "Wait!" Unlike his mortal self, Billy's ghost sounded rather sober.

Only then could James let out the breath that he'd been holding.

Georgia slipped under James' arm, her tears magically gone. "That was close."

Mother sobbed. "Is he...dead?"

Georgia went over to Billy's fallen form. She rolled it onto its back and studied it for a while. "No," Georgia replied. "However, he could be rather inconvenienced for a while. James? Fetch me that broken jug."

He complied. Yep, it was molasses. Not as bad as tar, but still unpleasantly sticky.

Holding it at arm's length so it wouldn't get on her gown, Georgia tipped the remains over Billy's body.

"What are you doing?" Mother cried out.

Georgia did not reply. She let it dribble over his face, his torso, along his limbs and everywhere until it was empty. Next, she fetched the feathers, dumping great armfuls over his sticky body. Then she sat down on a pew. "Now we wait." At her bidding, the curate fetched a damp handkerchief with which to wipe her sticky fingers.

It wasn't long until the ghost of Billy returned, contrite and trembling. Aunt Violet gasped and averted her eyes. Mother looked politely away.

"What have you done to me?" he wailed, his hands clenched in front of him because, as Georgia had been, he was stark naked.

Georgia confronted him. "You are now the Stoweham Ghost, to haunt and wander this village for as long as I please."

Dread filled his eyes. "You can't do that."

"Oh, yes I can." She knelt down by his body. "However, you have proven this ring is still dangerous. I cannot leave it in your possession, lest someone remove it from your finger and cause more mischief." She lifted Billy's good hand and pulled the ring from his sticky digit.

The ghost popped out of view. A moment later, Billy, now restored to his body, took a breath. He sat up, looked at his sticky, feathered self, and fled the chapel, like a scolded dog with his tail tucked between his legs.

Georgia wrapped the ring in the damp handkerchief.

Aunt Violet stood, her lips pursed. "He will never forgive you for this."

"I know," Georgia replied. "But by the time he's gotten over his embarrassment, James and I will be gone."

****

Once the rain eased up, Georgia talked Vicar

Johnson into loaning them his horse and buggy, with the curate to drive them to Buckingham train station. James and Georgia had packed the day before, not that they had much to their name.

Mother stood outside Stoweham House, a well-watered handkerchief wrung in her hands. "I will miss you so," she cried as she embraced her only son.

"You can come visit us in London," he replied, a touch of filial guilt tugging at his heart. If he had his way, he might not ever return to Stoweham, unless it was to facilitate the sale of the house. "Meanwhile, Mrs. Chelmscott's letter sounds promising. We'll write to you once we're established and you can tell me all about your good works." He sniffed. Wouldn't do to cry.

Georgia hugged her new mother-in-law. "Thank you for all you've done."

Mother held Georgia out at arm's length. "You will take good care of him, won't you?"

Georgia nodded.

So the new Mr. and Mrs. Cowper, formally of Stoweham, left the village where James had been born and Georgia had been imprisoned for a century. Not once did either of them turn around for a final glance at the place they once called home.

****

Later that afternoon James and Georgia stood on the Buckingham station platform, awaiting the one and only Sunday train to London. Other than the ticket seller hiding away from the weather in his wooden booth, they were blissfully alone. They had arrived with plenty of time to spare; the train was not due for another fifteen minutes. The rain had resumed, but the roof over the station platform kept them dry. As they stood there holding hands, Georgia hummed a tune, swaying in time to the music. James didn't recognize the tune.

"Neither do I," said Georgia. "It's been that long. But it played at the last dance I attended. I wanted to dance but hadn't been given permission."

He might not have known the tune, but he recognized the three-four time of a waltz. Pulling her hand to his shoulder, he held out his other hand for her. "Dance with me? After all, you are a married woman now."

Her face lit up with a smile. "Indeed I am."

This time, when James led in the steps of a waltz, Georgia had no problems following, her body pressed warmly to his.

"Promise me," she murmured into his ear, "that you'll dance with me now and always."

Joy filled James' heart. "I promise."

A word about the author…

Heidi Wessman Kneale is an Australian author of moderate repute best known for her escapist fiction. Like most humans, she has a family. She also associates with The World's Most Boring Cat. When not writing novels, she is a music composer and astronomer.

~*~

Find her online:
http://tinyurl.com/heidikneale/
@heidikneale

~*~

Other Heidi Wessman Kneale titles
available from The Wild Rose Press, Inc.:
MARRY ME
FOR RICHER, FOR POORER
AS GOOD AS GOLD